SAINT

Also by Ana Night

SAINT

SALVATION KINGS MC

ANA NIGHT

This is a work of fiction. All characters, names, places, and incidents are either the product of the author's imagination or are used fictitiously. Any resemblance to persons living or dead, business establishments, events or places is purely coincidental.

Cover content is for illustrative purposes only and any person depicted is a model.

Saint

Copyright © 2019 Ana Night

Digital ISBN: 123-0-00322-437-3
ISBN: 978-1-09770-947-2
ASIN: B07RN8Z3KJ
Second edition, April 2020

Chapter One
Zayne

THE SOUND of motorcycles nearing made Zayne perk up. It was the best sound in the world and it only got better because he knew it was his brothers coming. Five bikes rolled up in front of him. Zayne's best friend and the club's vice president, Joker, pulled off his helmet before walking to him. Joker had their sergeant at arms, two of their full-patch members, and a prospect with him.

"Saint," Joker said in greeting. "Where are they keeping them?"

"In the shed at the back of the property. There are only a chain-link fence and two guards between it and the road," Zayne said.

"Any ideas, prospect?" Joker asked.

The kid wasn't stupid. He knew Joker was testing him. Gabriel wasn't the least bit afraid of Joker. He should've been, though. Joker got his name because the only times he smiled was when he was beating the shit out of someone or killing them.

"I think we should use the sergeant as a distraction," Gabriel said.

Zayne tried hard not to smile, biting down on his lower lip.

Gabriel turned to the sergeant who was busy checking her nail polish and when she looked up at him, he said, "Let's be honest. You'd love it."

She smiled wryly at him. "Do I get to shoot people in this plan of yours?"

"As long as you keep them distracted, you can shoot whoever you want, Stiletto," Gabriel said.

She always wore high heels no matter what she was doing or where she was going. How she walked and even rode in those heels was a mystery to him. But they weren't the cause of her road name. The stiletto knives she always carried on her were. He'd seen her use them enough times to know not to piss her off.

"Good call, prospect," Joker said and turned to walk away. "Stay with the bikes."

Zayne saw the frustration clear on the kid's face, but he was smart enough to keep his trap shut. He should know by now that protesting Joker's orders wouldn't get him anywhere. Gabriel leaned back against his bike and crossed his arms over his chest, a sullen expression on his face. He looked longingly after Stiletto and the other two who were driving off on their bikes.

Zayne felt for Gabriel. The kid wanted to prove himself, but there was simply too much at stake for them to risk Gabriel screwing up. He gave Gabriel a stern look and turned to follow Joker. They were in York, Pennsylvania at another MC's clubhouse, because they'd stolen quite a few crates of weapons from the Kings and they were going to get them back. They were a klick from the edges of the Henchmen's property line, and they were making their way there on foot so the Henchmen wouldn't hear their bikes approaching from the back.

"We're gonna have to move fast," Zayne said. "I assume you have a way to get the crates out of here?"

Joker stopped and looked over his shoulder, a smile pulling at his lips and making Zayne fear his answer.

"Bandit's on his way with a van."

Zayne blinked at Joker and asked dubiously, "You let the guy who can barely ride his bike drive a van?"

"Don't worry." Joker turned back around and continued walking. "You get to drive it back. Bandit will take your bike."

Letting anyone else ride his bike felt like a violation and just the thought of Bandit defiling his girl made him see red. There was no way he was letting Bandit or anyone else near his bike.

"Why the fuck was I not involved in this decision?"

Joker made a snort-like sound before saying, "'Cause you pissed off before you could be a part of the decision making."

"I was following a lead. One that led me here," Zayne grumbled.

"What do you want? A medal or something?"

"Fuck off."

As soon as they neared the fence line of the property, they both fell silent and drew their guns. They moved together like they had in the army. It might have been years since they'd been discharged but being back on US soil hadn't changed how they worked together. They'd known each other since high school and they'd gone to boot camp together and then they'd been sent to war. They'd had each other's backs the whole time. They'd worked like a team for years, and they still did.

Joker held up a closed fist and they both came to a stop. Zayne could see the two guards past Joker's right side. They put their backs against the brick wall of a house and waited, keeping their eyes open and their ears peeled. Gunfire sounded from the front of the clubhouse. The two guards perked up but didn't leave their posts, which was unfortunate for them.

"We've gotta do this now," Joker said.

Zayne nodded. "Let's go get our property back."

Joker dipped his chin and with a hand, he instructed Zayne to stay put. Zayne obeyed and kept his gun aimed at the guards. He wanted to shoot these assholes for taking what wasn't theirs and he knew Joker did, too. He also knew his VP was trigger happy, especially in tense situations, so he needed to be Joker's voice of reason.

There was a small hole in the fence he'd found earlier when he'd been doing some recon of the place. Now they were making their way through it. It was a bit behind the shed so they could get in undetected. Joker gave him the signal to split up and Zayne walked to the other side of the shed so they could make their way to the front and the guards from each side.

He could still hear gunshots, but he knew it wouldn't be long before Stiletto and the others would need to retreat. The two guards were standing six feet from the shed, all their attention on listening to the gunfight. They never saw Joker and him coming. They each grabbed a man from behind, putting pressure on the sides of their necks to cut off the bloodstream. The man he was holding thrashed against him, but it was no use. He passed out and Zayne let him fall to the ground. They needed to work fast because save for killing the men, their only option was to lock them in the shed and they'd wake up soon enough.

He turned, covering Joker's back. When no one came running out of the main building, they went to the shed. Joker pushed down the handle and when nothing happened, he shook his head and stepped back to give Zayne room. Zayne kicked in the door and walked into the shed. A glance around made him breathe easier. The familiar crates filled the small space. He felt more than heard Joker walk up behind him and looked over his shoulder.

With a grin, he said, "Jackpot."

Nash

The excessive use of a car horn alerted him to his cousin's arrival. He grabbed his wallet and keys, shoving both into the inner pocket of his jacket. He was out the door, letting it slam and lock after him a few seconds later. He took the stairs two at a time, knowing he needed to hurry before Harper got annoyed and ended up pissing off all his neighbors.

Harper's red Toyota Yaris was parked at the curb, her window rolled down so she could yell at him to hurry up when she saw him. A smile teased his lips as he walked around the car to get into the passenger seat.

"Did you oversleep again?" Harper asked as she pulled the car back out onto the road.

"No. You're ten minutes early." He felt a grin form on his lips. "Eager much?"

"Shut up," Harper mumbled.

It was shit o'clock in the morning because they were on day shift at the firehouse where they worked, and Harper wasn't a morning person on a good day. Her being ten minutes early was solely because she hadn't seen her girlfriend in two days.

"You're coming Friday, right?"

Nash pulled a face even though she didn't see it.

"Why do I have to be at Mel's parents' wedding anniversary?"

Harper sighed. "Because it's *Mel's* parents anniversary."

"So?"

"She's your partner," Harper said, and he could practically hear her eyeroll.

"Yeah, but now she's your partner, too."

"Are you jealous?"

"No, I'm just tired because all she talks about is you. Guess who she comes to for advice on you? Me."

Harper scrunched up her nose and said, "That's not good."

"I know," Nash said with a deep sigh.

It was downright horrible. Him giving advice on his cousin, who also happened to be a woman, just wasn't going to end well. Anything he said had a possibility of coming back to bite him in the ass later.

The drive to their firehouse in Fells Point didn't take more than fifteen minutes and when Harper parked the car, Nash caught sight of a few of their coworkers in the parking lot. Caleb was standing outside, fumbling with his phone, and Nash wasn't surprised when Harper made her way toward him, dragging Nash with her.

"Hey, Caleb. Can you please explain to Nash why he needs to go to Mel's parents anniversary," Harper said.

Caleb's head shot up, his eyes wide. Caleb opened his mouth, then shut it and shook his head.

"Did she bully you into going as well?" Nash asked.

Caleb nodded, a defeated expression on his face. The guy was a bit of a push-over when it came to Harper. They'd been best friends since high school so Harper knew exactly which buttons to push to get him to do what she wanted.

"Tony's coming too," Caleb mumbled, speaking of his partner.

Nash patted Caleb on the back of his shoulder while giving the man a pitying look.

"At least there'll be booze," Nash said with a sigh.

Caleb nodded and said, "That's the only reason *I'm* going. That and Tony's forcing me."

"You two suck," Harper said and flipped them both off.

"Dick maybe," Nash said under his breath.

From the wide grin spreading on Caleb's face, he'd heard him. Nash shook his head and pushed at Caleb's shoulder. Caleb chuckled as he stumbled backward. They walked into the garage where he saw Mel sitting in the driver's seat of the ambulance, the door open as she talked to Paul, one of the firefighters. Harper made her way toward Mel while Caleb and Nash continued inside to the locker room.

They passed a few of the firefighters from the night shift on their way and they all looked tired as hell. They found their lieutenant sitting on the bench, getting into his uniform. They changed clothes while listening to Lieutenant Fletcher talk about his daughter's upcoming baseball game. They both promised to be there to cheer on Kelly. Every time they had a weekend shift, Kelly and her mother showed up with baked goods. Kelly was a sweet and smart girl who loved being at the firehouse as much as they loved having her there.

The alarm went off and the second he knew it was for him and Mel, he cursed and took off into the garage. He ran to the ambulance and as soon as his door slammed behind him, Mel put her foot on the speeder.

"You're coming to my parents anniversary party, right?" Mel asked.

Nash held back a groan and said, "Of course, I am. You're my partner."

"She's forcing you, isn't she?"

Nash snorted out a laugh. Of course, Mel saw right through him.

"You don't have to come if you don't want to, Nash."

"You know damned well I'll be there because you're the one who asked," he said. He meant it, too. He sighed. "Everything would be so much easier if you weren't screwing my cousin."

"True that."

They shared a quick smile before they both turned their attention back on the road. Nash sat up straight when they neared the address. Mel pulled over and they got out of the ambulance, grabbing their gear as they went. They walked up to a big iron gate and when they found it locked, they peeked through the bars. A group of people were standing in a circle and Nash guessed their patient would be in the middle.

"Did somebody call for a medic?" Mel yelled.

A few heads turned their way. Some started arguing but no one came to let them in.

"I think we might need some assistance," Mel said.

Nash bobbed his head and let her make the call. He tried to assess the scene. The men were wearing leather cuts with something printed on the back. A row of motorcycles was lined up on one side. This could definitely turn bad fast.

Mel cursed and said, "Something's wrong with my 'talkie."

Nash frowned and tried his own but got nothing but static.

"Shit. I'm gonna run to the ambo real quick," Mel said. "Don't you dare go in there without me."

He nodded absently, a set of bright green eyes having caught his attention. The face and body that went with those eyes made his brain stall for a long moment while the man walked up to the gate, a scowl on his face.

"You have to let us in," Nash said.

"You need to leave. We don't want cops here," the biker said.

"If you don't hurt us, we won't need any cops."

The biker looked indecisive, which worked for him. He might not need more than a little push.

"Please. Your friend is hurt. Let us help him," Nash said.

With a groan, the biker shook his head and stepped back, opening the gate by typing in a code on the keypad off to the left.

"Mel," Nash yelled over his shoulder. "Get back here and cancel the backup."

With the gate open, he stepped inside.

"Thank you," Nash said as he followed the biker. "I'm Nash, by the way."

"Saint."

Nash was baffled for a second, not expecting to get a name like that. Then again, the guy was a biker. There was nothing normal about him. As they neared the group of people, he noticed a pair of feet on the ground, which meant his patient was in the middle of seven, huge biker guys. On the back of their vests was an image of a skull wearing a crown and 'Salvation Kings' written above it.

"Hey, I need you all to move back," Nash yelled.

Not a single one of them reacted.

"You heard him. Move," Saint growled.

It had the desired effect. People scrambled to get away. Only one stayed. An older woman sat on the ground with the man's head in her lap. Nash kneeled down and put his bag on the ground. The man was fortunately conscious.

"Hello, sir. My name is Nash. Can you tell me what's happening?"

"I'm having a heart attack that's what's happening," the man grumbled.

"Oh, stop it. Just tell him what you're feeling," the woman said.

Nash glanced up at her while taking the man's pulse.

"I'm Nancy and this grumpy bear is Anders," she said with a fond look at the man.

"My chest and my left arm hurts. I got dizzy and tripped over myself. Auggie, that dumbass, tried to catch me," Anders said and glared at someone behind Nash. "I weigh more than the double of you, squirt."

"I went down with him, but I cushioned his head."

Nash glanced to his left where a smaller, blond guy was standing, holding one of his hands against his chest. Blood ran from his knuckles. Nash returned his attention to his patient while saying, "Get that checked and don't shake it."

Auggie mumbled a, "Yes, sir."

"Do you have any history of chest pain or heart conditions?" Nash asked as he worked to get Anders' shirt open, so he could place electrodes on his chest to take an ECG. Luckily, Anders didn't have a lot of chest hair.

"The only chest pain he gets is from beating on it so much," Nancy said.

Mel showed up with the stretcher then. She crouched down on the other side of Anders, saying, "Talk to me."

"Possible MI. Starting the ECG now," Nash said.

It only took a moment for it to start up. One look at the monitor and Mel said, "Let's get him in the ambo."

Nash gave a nod of agreement and glanced over Mel's shoulder. His eyes met Saint's and he asked, "You mind giving us a hand?"

Nash had a feeling Anders would much rather accept help from Saint and he'd need it if he was to get on the stretcher. Saint gave him a nod and put his arms under Anders' shoulders. Together they got Anders onto the stretcher and then they were off to the ambulance. Once the stretcher and Anders were in the ambulance, Nash gave Nancy a hand to help her up the step before getting in himself. Mel was already behind the wheel so all he needed to do was close the doors. Before he could do anything, though, Saint was there, closing one door and just before he closed the other, his green eyes locked with Nash's.

"Thank you," Nash said.

Saint gave him a short nod and closed the door.

Zayne

Watching the ambulance drive off with Grizz and Nancy felt wrong. As much as he wanted to drive after them, he knew he needed to stick around and make sure no one did anything stupid. Some of his brothers were easily riled and the last thing they needed was them beating on each other.

He walked into the clubhouse, heading straight for the bar. The sergeant was already there plundering the liquor cabinet. She looked up when she heard him and raised a bottle of Jack Daniel's toward him. At his nod, she grinned and closed the cabinet door. She grabbed two tumblers and set them and the bottle on the bar.

"One hell of a way to start the day, huh?"

She poured them both a generous amount and when he grabbed his glass, she clinked her own with his and threw back the whiskey. He raised a brow at her and grinned when she shot him a wink. Addison "Stiletto" Parish wasn't an average woman. She could drink more than most of the guys in the club and she was strong-willed and tough as all hell. When she spoke, everyone listened because they knew the consequences of ignoring her. She upheld the laws in the club, and everyone had great respect for both them and her.

Zayne took a sip of his whiskey. He'd never been a day-drinker but watching Grizz go down like that made the alcohol seem much more appealing.

"You think he'll be okay?" Addison asked, concern showing on her face.

"I think he's one hell of a fighter and he'll have the hospital staff wanting to kick him and his filthy mouth out in no time," Zayne said.

Her lips quirked into a smile. "That's true."

Zayne smiled at her and took another sip. Addison filled her own glass again.

"That paramedic was something else. That gorgeous face and all that dark, delicious skin. I bet his body is just as mouthwatering," Addison said with a pointed look at Zayne.

He'd noticed the eyes first. They were a golden brown and the second they'd caught Zayne's gaze, he'd known he was in trouble. Nash's voice was soft yet demanding and he seemed completely sincere. Nash had brown skin and full lips which Zayne would be dreaming about for days. He was about two inches shorter than Zayne with a lean body and he was probably hiding a fair bit of muscle under that uniform. His head was shaved, making Zayne wonder if the rest of the hair on his body was as well. He desperately wanted to find out.

"I don't know what you're talking about," he said.

"The only people who say that are people who know exactly what you're talking about."

Zayne shook his head and sighed. He turned his back to her and leaned against the bar, his glass hanging from his fingertips. She always knew things she wasn't supposed to. Saw things no one else did.

"Maybe," he said.

Addison grunted and he sighed when he heard her get up onto the bar top. She sat next to him with her legs hanging over the edge. She nudged his arm with her knee, making him look at her.

"Maybe? That's all you've got?" She shook her head, something like outrage on her face. "Babe, even I wanted to fuck him, and I don't do older guys."

He couldn't help but snort at that. "He's probably younger than me."

He didn't consider his thirty-one years that old.

"Yeah, but you know I like them barely legal," Addison said, twirling a blonde strand of hair around a finger while she batted her lashes at him.

He was only three years older than her, but she didn't date anyone over the age of twenty-two. She'd once told him she liked them young and eager to prove themselves.

Agitated voices coming from behind him, made him glance over his shoulder. He saw Rooster, one of the full patched members, get in a prospect named Jordan's face, yelling and pushing him. Jordan threw his hands up and said something that made Rooster take a swing at him. Jordan ducked and moved back, staying out of Rooster's reach, but Zayne couldn't let it continue. With a sigh, he pushed away from the bar.

"Rooster. Knock it off," he growled as he neared.

Rooster turned his gaze on Zayne, saying, "This little bitch was talking shit about Grizz."

"Was not," Jordan mumbled, his gaze of his feet.

Zayne sighed. He was doing that a lot today.

"Jordan, go keep Stiletto company," he said.

Jordan didn't need to be told twice. He turned on his heels and headed toward Addison with bounce in his strides. He had a hard-on for her, or he should say, a *crush* on her. The guy was smitten but Addison didn't spare him as much as a glance. He was twenty-six which made him too old in her eyes. Jordan was a kind man. Too sweet he sometimes thought. He wasn't sure what Jordan was doing with them. They were a rowdy bunch and danger was a prominent part of their lifestyle. It didn't fit with the shy and gentle man, but something told him Jordan wouldn't have a problem with the dangerous parts. There was more to him than what met the eye. He was sure of it.

Zayne turned strict eyes on Rooster and said, "Keep it clean today. We don't need another ambulance here."

Rooster got an embarrassed look on his face and agreed in a hoarse voice. The guy had one hell of a temper on him, but he respected authority and orders better than most. Especially from his old lady. Even if no one else could get through to him, she always managed to do it.

The sound of motorcycles made everyone perk up. A few of the guys headed outside and Zayne followed. He watched from the door as their president, King, brought his bike to a stop at the end of the row of bikes. Gabriel pulled up next to him. They'd been gone on a two day's ride. King's old lady and the mother of his two kids came walking out of the garage. A wide, toothy grin filled King's face as he walked toward her. Polly was backing away, waving a wrench at him but that didn't deter him one bit. King had her thrown over his shoulder the next second. They disappeared into the garage, probably headed toward King's office in there. Some of the guys were whistling and cat-calling and when the door closed behind King and Polly, they turned their attention to Gabriel. They teased him about his parents, but he just waved them off with a laugh.

Zayne shook his head, a smile finding his lips when Gabriel flipped off Bones. Zayne walked into the courtyard, heading for his bike. He bent down to check the front tire. He needed to take her to the shop so he could get the tires changed. Lennox, Rooster's old lady, was the head mechanic of the club's auto repair shop and she was the best they had. She would take good care of his girl.

"Hey. I just heard," Gabriel said, walking up next to Zayne.

Zayne straightened up and turned to look at Gabriel. Concern was evident on the kid's face. Gabriel must have known Grizz most of his life, so he could understand the kid being affected by what had happened.

"How is he?"

"I don't know. I haven't heard anything from Nancy yet, but he was talking and being his grumpy old self when they drove off to the hospital."

They heard a yelp, and both turned in time to see a red-faced Auggie rush out of the garage. He was still cradling his hand, but he'd wrapped it in a washcloth now. The outraged look on his face gave Zayne a good idea of what Auggie had just walked in on. Auggie headed toward Zayne and Gabriel.

"Why do I always forget to knock?" Auggie asked with a groan.

Gabriel chuckled and a smile pulled at Zayne's lips.

Auggie narrowed his eyes at Gabriel and said, "Or better yet, you should teach your old man to put a damned sock on the door."

"Experience has taught me not to try and change my dad. He is one old dog you cannot teach any new tricks and if you try—"

Auggie cut him off with a wave and said, "Yeah. Yeah. I got it. Teach your mom to do it, then."

Gabriel burst into laughter, shaking his head at Auggie.

"I'll let you do that yourself. I have to go pick up my sister from school. Pop found out she's been to a party while we were gone so she's grounded, she just doesn't know it yet," Gabriel said.

"I'm sure that'll go over well," Auggie said.

Gabriel sighed, closing his eyes and shaking his head.

"I've told pops to let her be, but you know how he gets. He still hasn't learned that if he tells her not to do something, she's definitely going to do it."

"Good luck with that," Zayne said.

"Thanks. Knowing my sister, I'll need it."

They watched Gabriel walk back to his bike, stop in front of it, and then shake his head before heading toward one of the cars parked in the courtyard. That seemed like a good idea. No way was he going to get Dara on the back of his bike. He'd heard her flat out tell her parents that if she was ever getting on a bike, she would be the one driving it. Zayne had a smile on his lips until he glanced down at Auggie's still bloody hand.

"Let's get that checked out," Zayne said.

He started toward his bike but was brought short by Auggie's outraged gasp. He turned to a scandalized looking Auggie.

"First of all, I'm not riding bitch. Second, I can't hold on with one hand."

"I see you've got your priorities in order," Zayne said with an amused grin.

Auggie flipped him off with his good hand.

Zayne laughed and reached into his jeans pocket to pull out the keys to one of the cars.

Chapter Two

Nash

NASH PUT the last bag of groceries into the shopping cart and waited for Mel to pay. It was their turn to cook and buy groceries for the firehouse. Whenever they did a grocery run, they always made sure to buy enough for the four days they'd be working so they didn't have to go out several times.

When Mel was done, he pushed the cart toward the exit. They were just walking out the doors when Mel came to an abrupt halt.

"Shit. I forgot the Lieutenant's sugar-free stuff," Mel said. She turned and over her shoulder, she yelled, "I'll be right back."

He shook his head and kept walking. He was halfway across the parking lot when someone called his name. Nash turned around and stared. The biker—the one with the green eyes who'd let them in—was walking toward him. He wasn't sure if he should be afraid or not. The man was imposing with his height and wide shoulders, the stubble on his chin, his intense eyes and that leather cut. The man looked dangerous but who was he kidding? It only made him sexier.

Saint stopped in front of him, an easy smile on his lips.

"I never got to thank you."

Nash blinked at him.

"You saved his life," Saint said.

"Well, you're quite welcome. It is sort of my job," Nash said.

Saint shook his head. "You could've easily walked away. We weren't exactly being forthcoming, and most people are scared of us."

He didn't know what to say to that so he kept his mouth shut. Saint extended his hand and said, "I'm Zayne."

"Nash," he said and cringed. Zayne already knew that.

He shook Zayne's hand and butterflies decided to invade his stomach. He didn't think he'd ever been this nervous around a guy before. Or any person for that matter. There was just something about the way those impossibly green eyes were watching him.

"Hey, dumbass, are we going or not?" was yelled from a car parked near them.

"Shut it, Auggie," Zayne yelled back.

He caught sight of the guy who'd hurt his hand trying to catch Anders. He was looking a lot better and he certainly wasn't as timid as he'd been earlier.

"How's his hand? Did he get it checked out?"

Zayne nodded. "Yeah. We've just come from the hospital. He busted his knuckles and sprained his wrist and two fingers."

Nash jumped when Auggie was suddenly standing next to them.

"It fucking sucks. I can't ride," Auggie said.

"Guess you'll have to ride bitch anyway," Zayne said with a smirk.

"Fuck no," Auggie blurted. "The cages are automatic."

Nash looked between them, confusion causing a frown to form on his forehead.

"What's a cage?"

"A car," Zayne explained.

Nash raised an eyebrow. "Why not just call it a car, then?"

Auggie chuckled and with a slap to Zayne's shoulder, he turned around and said, "Good luck explaining that."

Nash looked up at Zayne expectantly.

Zayne shook his head and said, "It's not important. I'll explain some other time."

He liked the sound of that. If Zayne thought they'd see each other again, it probably wasn't because he was expecting to need a medic soon. Or maybe it was. Either way, he knew he had to take a chance that it was the former.

"Give me your phone."

Zayne looked skeptical for all of two seconds before unlocking and placing his phone in Nash's hand. He didn't know why he did it, but it felt right. He entered his number into the phone and handed it back to Zayne.

"My number. If you have any questions or if you ever need a paramedic again."

"Thank you," Zayne said, holding the phone up as he walked backward.

Zayne turned around and Nash watched him walk back to his car—cage, or whatever—and get behind the wheel. Zayne raised a hand as he drove past Nash. His eyes followed the car until it disappeared from sight.

"What the hell are you doing still standing here?" Mel asked, making him jump. He hadn't heard her walk up behind him.

"No reason. Let's get going," he said, shaking his head to try and clear it.

Zayne

He'd dropped Auggie off at his apartment with one bag of groceries. The rest was for someone else and as he drove the twenty minutes to her house, he replayed his conversation with Nash over and over again. The guy was definitely interested, and Zayne admired him for his courage. There weren't many people who would talk to a biker, let alone give one their number. Especially if they were a guy. There was something special about the man. Something that had drawn him in from the first time their eyes met. He wasn't sure what it was, but he knew he wanted to find out.

He parked on the street and grabbed the grocery bags from the trunk. He walked up the stone path to the front door, throwing a glance over his shoulder to see if anyone was watching him. There was always one King here, watching out for Talyssa.

He knocked on the door and waited even though he had a key. He didn't like to invade her space by just walking right in. He heard footsteps on the other side of the door and then the click of the locks. The door swung open to reveal a dark-haired, five foot six inches tall, pregnant woman. A big smile widened her lips.

"Zayne."

"Hi, doll," he said and held up the grocery bags. "I've got your groceries."

"Oh, thank you," she said and stepped aside to let him walk in.

You couldn't see it on her, but she carried many deep scars on her soul. Talyssa was the sweetest and kindest woman he'd ever met. The thought of anyone wanting to hurt her, her husband of all people, was almost surreal to him.

"Nic's here, too," Talyssa said.

"Really?"

Talyssa nodded, a sweet smile spreading on her lips. "Yeah. He's putting the crib together. Or trying to, I should say."

Zayne chuckled and shook his head. If Nic was here he'd probably sent whoever had been watching Talyssa home, knowing she hated keeping them from the other things they could be doing instead of watching over her. He walked with Talyssa to the kitchen where he helped her with the groceries and then he made his way to the nursery. He stopped in the doorway, leaning a shoulder against the doorframe. Nic, better known as Hawk in the club, was sitting on the floor surrounded by white parts of the still unassembled crib. He looked utterly lost as he held up one piece and grimaced.

"Need some help there, Hawk?"

Hawk glanced up at him. "Please."

Zayne grinned and walked across the room to sit down next to him. He grabbed the instructions manual, took one look at it and threw it away. He reached for the biggest piece but was halted by Talyssa's voice coming from the doorway.

"Ya'll want some coffee or something else to drink?" Talyssa asked.

"You got vodka?" Hawk asked.

Zayne shook his head and looked up at Talyssa, saying, "Coffee's fine, thank you."

She smiled at him before disappearing back into the hallway. Hawk's eyes were following Talyssa, a sappy look on his face. It was somewhat disconcerting. Hawk was usually more the silent brooding type.

"Why are you so happy?" Zayne asked.

Hawk shrugged and sat up. "I just like being here."

"So you don't like being at the club?"

"Fuck off."

That was more like it.

Talyssa came back with a cup of coffee in each hand. Zayne took his from her with a thankful smile. It took them the better part of an hour but once they were done, Talyssa had a functioning crib for her baby. She was due in three weeks and from the looks of it, Hawk was much more stressed out about it than she was. Zayne hadn't exactly been around pregnant ladies a lot, but he was convinced Talyssa was taking everything much calmer than most.

"Do you guys wanna stay for dinner? I'm just about to throw something together," Talyssa said.

Zayne shook his head. "Thank you for the offer, but I should get going." He threw a glance at Hawk. "But I think this one could do with a homecooked meal."

Hawk was one big smile as he told Talyssa he'd love to stay.

"All right. I'll let myself out," Zayne said and pushed up off the floor.

"Thank you for the groceries and for stopping by to help," Talyssa said.

He wrapped his arms around her in a tight hug and said, "Anytime, doll."

He said goodbye to Hawk and walked to the door which he made sure to lock after himself. He went to the car and just as he got in, his phone rang. He dug his phone out of his jeans pocket with a groan and considered hanging up until he saw who the caller was.

"Hi, Em."

"Hey, big bro. Long time no talk," Emery said.

Zayne snorted and said, "We talked, like, two days ago."

Emery's contagious laughter sounded through the phone, making him smile. He turned on the car and connected his phone so he could talk while he drove.

"What's up, Em?"

"Joker called. He said Grizz is in the hospital?"

"Yeah," Zayne said on a sigh. "I'm on my way to check on him and Nancy right now."

"Will you tell them I called?"

"Of course. They'd probably both like to hear your voice," he said.

"I'd like that too. Just, please, only call me on your phone. I don't wanna get in trouble for calling a *gang member*."

The sarcasm in Emery's voice when she said it made him roll his eyes. Some people called motorcycle clubs gangs and every single biker he knew hated it.

"Whatever the princess wants," he quipped.

"Jerk," Emery said. "How are you? Really?"

"I'm fine, Em."

"Fuck you. Don't you dare try that shit with me. I know you better than anyone."

"I'm not brushing you off. I mean it. I am fine. Of course, I'm worried about Grizz, but I'm good. I swear."

"Good. 'Cause if you aren't, you know I'll just hear it from Joker."

Zayne shook his head, his lips quirking at the corners. His sister wasn't someone you messed with. She might be five years younger than him but that certainly hadn't stopped her from hanging around Joker and him when they were younger. She'd followed them to the Kings years ago when she was still in college. He knew she'd loved being around the club, but she'd never been a member and when she got a job offer as the security office administrator in the Senate, no one had the slightest problem letting her go. They all hated to see her leave, but he knew they all wanted her to be happy, even if that entailed her not being able to speak with or see anyone apart from Zayne and occasionally Joker. He knew Gabriel had taken it the hardest. The two of them had been very close.

"You know I'd never lie to you," Zayne said and meant every word.

"I know," Emery said with a sigh. "It's just… Not being there, it just sucks sometimes."

"You're living your dream, Em. I know it's hard, I know that some days you just wanna come home, but you're amazing at what you do, and you deserve to give this a shot."

"Thanks, Zayne. For always being there for me," Emery said.

"You're very welcome. Just remember to get me that 'best brother in the world' mug for my birthday, all right?"

"Sure, whatever," Emery said, laughter in her voice.

"I'm not kidding. Also, I'm pulling up at the hospital now. I'll call you once I'm inside, okay?"

"Yeah. I'll talk to you soon. Bye."

Emery hung up and Zayne circled the parking lot a few times before he found a spot. He got out of the car and made his way to the hospital entrance. Nancy had texted him earlier with a floor and room number. He found it easily enough and when he walked into the room, it was to find Grizz lying in the bed, hooked up to a monitor. He looked as grumpy as ever, though he did also look like he was doing better.

"Saint," Grizz said, his voice gravelly.

"Hey, brother. How are you?"

Grizz tried to sit up and cursed when he couldn't get up.

"Take it easy," Zayne said and walked to Grizz's side.

"That's what they all say," Grizz grumbled.

"Who? The doctors?"

"Them and Nancy."

"That's 'cause you need to relax, you buffoon," came from the doorway.

Zayne looked up to see Nancy standing there, an exasperated look on her face. She said hello to Zayne and chided Grizz some more before sitting down in a chair by the bed and taking Grizz's hand.

"Em called," Zayne said, getting their attention. "She wants to speak with you both."

Nancy lit up at the sound of Emery's name. "Really?"

"Yeah. Here," he said and handed her his phone. "Use that to call her. Imma go see if I can find some food in this place."

"Thank you," Grizz said.

He left them to it and went in search of the cafeteria.

Chapter Three

Nash

"YOU KEEP looking at your phone like that and I might end up thinking I'm boring you," Ford said.

Nash looked up from his phone, embarrassment burning on his cheeks. He slid the phone into his jeans pocket. He'd been waiting for Zayne to call since Monday. He'd waited five days and by now he should've come to terms with the fact Zayne wasn't going to call.

"Sorry," he said.

"Don't be. If someone's got you that distracted, they've gotta be something special, right?"

"Right."

He nodded and raised his beer to his lips. He didn't know how Mel had managed to cajole the police officer to come to her parents' party. He hadn't even known they were friends. Sure they met from time to time courtesy of their jobs, but he'd never seen them together outside of work. She'd never mentioned they were friends, but she had a big heart and perhaps she'd invited him because she knew he was having a hard time and might need some people around him.

Ford only had one year on the job. It'd been one hell of a year, though. His former training officer turned out to be on the take and he'd kidnapped a homicide detective's kids to make her kill one of her colleagues. Before that, the asshole had shot and almost killed Nash's best friend's boyfriend. The bastard even tried to kill him again at the hospital but almost got Nash's best friend instead. They were both alright, though, and he was now in jail, awaiting trial.

Nash turned his gaze on Ford when a thought struck him. "Hey, what do you know about the Salvation Kings motorcycle club?"

One of Ford's brows almost hit his hairline. "Why?"

Nash shrugged and tried to play it off like it wasn't anything important, saying, "We got a call to their place a few days ago. I was just curious."

"You and the whole police department," Ford said. "We don't actually know a whole lot about them. They've got a few legit businesses but that one percent patch on their cuts tells a different story."

"What do you mean?"

"There are a lot of law-abiding motorcycle clubs around but just about one percent of them are criminals. That's why they wear that patch. It's to let people know they're outlaws and not to mess with them."

"I don't remember hearing anything about them in the news," Nash said.

"Bikers are generally hard to convict. People are afraid to testify against them and they're smart about how they run their club," Ford said, shaking his head. "But the Kings are especially good at staying under the radar. I guess it might have to do with a lot of their members being former military."

Nash nodded to himself, his thoughts whirring a bit. He'd known they were dangerous when he'd been inside the club's gates, but he'd also gotten the sense that they were people who cared deeply about each other. Not that one excluded the other, of course.

Caleb sat down in the chair next to Ford, a deep sigh escaping him.

"And I thought *my* family was crazy," Caleb said.

Tony walked up behind Caleb, putting his hands on the back of his chair and leaning down to press a kiss to Caleb's cheek. "Babe, your family is amazing."

Caleb tsked and shook his head, saying, "You only think that because they love you more than me."

"That may very well be true," Tony said with a smug smile.

Nash sat back in his chair, drinking his beer as he watched his friends tease each other. They were a good bunch, that was for sure. He loved having them in his life and he knew they'd all welcome Ford with open arms. That was just the kind of people they were.

Zayne

He was staring off into space when his phone vibrated. For a split-second, he thought it might be Nash, but then he remembered he hadn't actually given the guy his number. Disappointment started to creep in, but he shoved it back down. The text was from his sister, asking about Grizz. He typed out a short answer and sent off the message. He tightened his grip on the phone, his teeth grinding. He had no idea what to do about Nash. Obviously, he wanted the guy to reach out, but he was the only one with the means to do that and he'd been fighting himself on the issue for way too many days now.

"Whatever that phone has done to you it must be pretty bad with the way you're glaring at it," Addison said as she sat down across from Zayne. He glanced up at her with a frown and then let out a breath when her words registered. He put his phone face-down on the table.

"Is it that paramedic? Does he not want to see you?"

"No, it's…" Zayne shook his head. "Well, yes. It is him, but I don't know if he'll want to see me."

"Why?"

"He gave me his number and I—"

"Whoa. Stop right there. He gave you his number? And you think he *doesn't* want to see you?"

He arched an eyebrow at her, but she simply crossed her arms and leaned back in her seat, a smile playing on her lips.

"You're being an idiot," she said.

"He's a paramedic."

"So?"

Zayne shook his head and said, "So, he could probably get fired for just knowing me."

Two of their prospects, Jordan and Maya, walked up to their table, making Zayne clamp his mouth shut.

"Ya'll talking 'bout that paramedic?" Maya asked as she sat down in the chair next to Addison.

Zayne rolled his eyes and said, "Why does everyone know about that?"

"Because Bandit's got a big mouth," Jordan said.

Zayne looked up at Jordan, his eyes narrowing as he turned his head to the side.

"Auggie blabbed?"

Jordan nodded his head eagerly.

"That piece of shit," Zayne grumbled though there was no real heat behind the words. If he hadn't wanted people to know, he shouldn't have told Auggie that Nash gave him his number. Auggie wasn't the least bit good at keeping his trap shut.

He wasn't entirely sure how Auggie ended up with Bandit as his road name, but he did know how he'd ended up with the nickname Band-Aid. He was their treasurer, but he usually did everything from a computer so how the idiot got all his papercuts was a mystery to him. He was always getting his fingertips cut so the first month he'd been a prospect, he'd usually been asking people for band-aids until he ended up carrying a pack on himself.

The door slammed open and in came Hawk, dragging a body behind him. Zayne wasn't exactly surprised. He'd seen a lot of crazy shit both in the army and after joining the club, but Hawk was a whole other level. You never really knew where you had him.

"Somebody carry this dipshit upstairs," Hawk yelled.

"Prospects," Zayne said with a motion of his hand toward Hawk.

They both stood and made their way over there, Jordan grabbing the guy's feet while Maya put her arms under his shoulders. Zayne watched them carry the man toward the stairs and then he turned his attention on Hawk who was just sitting down next to Addison.

"He alive?" Zayne asked.

Hawk turned a grin his way and said, "Barely."

"Who is he?"

Hawk reached down to lift a bag up onto the table. Zayne stared at him when he pulled out a Devil's Henchmen cut.

"They're here?"

Hawk nodded. "Yeah. That's why I caught this bastard."

If the Henchmen were in Baltimore, then they had to be up to something big. They'd need that guy to spill all the Henchmen secrets he knew.

"First, they steal our property and now they're here? You should think they'd learned their lesson after the way we left them the last time," Zayne said with a shake of his head.

"Do we know how they found our stash yet?" Hawk asked.

Addison shook her head. "I'm still hoping they simply stumbled over it."

Neither Zayne nor Hawk said anything to that. He wasn't sure about Hawk, but he was hoping the Henchmen finding their stash was a coincidence because if it wasn't it meant someone sold them out. Someone close enough to know where they kept it.

Hawk's phone rang and while he answered, Zayne turned his attention to Addison.

"Have you heard anything from King?"

Addison shook her head and said, "No. He hasn't said a word about it. I think he's hoping for the best but preparing for the worst. He hasn't said it out loud, but I think he's got someone looking into it."

"Auggie," Zayne guessed.

"Probably."

As it was, Auggie would be King's best shot at finding something out. Auggie wasn't just their treasurer, he was one hell of a hacker, too. Before he'd come to them, he'd gotten himself into a shitty situation because of his skill set and it had taken much more than hacking to get him out of it. But they'd come through for him and now he was one of them.

"Fuck," Hawk hissed and turned to Zayne with a panicked look in his eyes. "Talyssa is going into labor."

"But Doc's outta town," Zayne said, not truly understanding the meaning of Hawk's words.

"I know," Hawk growled. He ran his hands through his hair. "What the fuck are we gonna do? She's not due for another two weeks."

"Take a deep breath, big guy," Addison said, reaching out to pat his arm.

Hawk scowled at her but did as she said. Addison waited until he was calmer before she asked, "Did she say anything about her water breaking? How close the contractions are?"

"She said her water just broke," Hawk said.

"Alright. That means she's actually in labor and not just having Braxton Hicks. You should get over there."

"How do you know those things?" Zayne asked.

Addison shrugged and said, "I was with my cousin both times she went into labor. You learn a thing or two."

Zayne shook his head at her in wonder. He'd never have taken her for someone who'd willingly participate in a birth. Hawk headed toward the door, so Zayne grabbed his phone and followed. As they walked to their motorcycles, Hawk kept trying to call the doctor but from the growly sounds coming from him, the doc wasn't picking up.

"Fucking hell. We're gonna have to deliver the damned baby ourselves. I'm not equipped for something like this."

"Neither am I, brother," Zayne said.

He grabbed his helmet but before he could put it on, a thought made him pause.

"I know someone I can call," Zayne said.

Hawk got a somewhat relieved look on his face and said, "Do it."

Nash

The car came to a stop in front of a small, one-story house. There was what looked like a newer detached garage and a beautiful flower bed out front. It didn't look like a place a biker would live. But what the hell did he know?

"Thanks for the lift, Ford." He held up Ford's first-aid kit. "And for this."

Ford gave him a nod. "Anytime."

Nash got out and walked around the car to the sidewalk. He waved to Ford and watched him pull back out onto the road, then he turned and made his way to the front door. He raised his fist to knock but before he could, the door opened. He took a second to just take in the man in front of him. Zayne was wearing a faded pair of jeans and a black t-shirt that clung to his chest. His dark hair was in disarray as if he'd run his hands through it one too many times.

"Nash," Zayne said with a relieved sigh.

"Hi."

He swallowed hard at the intensity in Zayne's eyes as he looked Nash over. Nash shifted from one foot to the other and cleared his throat, arching a brow at Zayne.

Zayne stepped back to let him in and closed the door after him.

"So, what am I—"

He was cut off by a yell coming from further inside the house. He turned wide eyes on Zayne who grimaced and motioned for him to follow. He was led down a hallway until they made it to a bedroom where Zayne stopped and moved aside to let Nash walk ahead of him. A woman was sitting on a bed, a blanket covering her spread legs. A man was sitting next to her, holding one of her hands. It was clear from the expression on the woman's face that she was in pain. Something else was also becoming clear to him.

"She's having a baby," Nash mumbled. He turned on his heels to glare at Zayne. "She needs an obstetrician. I'm a paramedic. I've never delivered a baby."

He knew other paramedics who had, because sometimes babies just decided that now was the time. He knew Mel had done it at least once, but he hadn't even witnessed a real birth before.

"I know you can do this. She needs you," Zayne said.

"She needs a hospital," Nash muttered.

"She can't risk going to one."

The woman began screaming and his drive to help people was kicking in full force, but he kept his feet firmly planted on the ground. He wasn't moving until he got some more information.

"Look. I wouldn't have asked you to come if I could see any other way. She can't go to the hospital because her husband would find out and he'd—" Zayne shook his head, a grim expression crossing his face. "He'll kill her and the baby, okay?"

"What? Are you serious?"

Zayne nodded.

"That's when you call the police."

"They know, and they say they can't help her unless she's got proof that he wants to hurt her, which she can't get before he actually hurts her. Besides, most of them are on the take."

"Jesus fucking Christ," Nash spat. "This is not what I meant when I said you could call me."

"Look, I'm sorry, but she really needs your help. *I* need your help," Zayne said.

There was a vulnerability to Zayne's words and a desperate look in his eyes. Nash sighed and said, "You're so gonna owe me dinner for this," before walking into the bedroom. He walked to the bed, stopping at the woman's side. He put the kit down next to her and leaned down.

"Hi. I'm Nash. I'm a paramedic. What's your name?"

"Talyssa," she said between gasps.

The guy holding Talyssa's hand looked like he wanted to kill someone when another contraction hit her and she began panting, then cried out. He turned a dark, deadly glare on Nash.

"Can't you give her something for the pain?"

"I'm not a walking pharmacy," Nash hissed. "God damn it. I came here from a fucking party. I've been drinking and all I have with me is my friend's first-aid kit from his car. Don't expect miracles from me."

"Can you help her or not?"

"Yes. I'll help her. But I need you to breathe with her, can you do that?"

The guy nodded and turned his attention on Talyssa. Nash breathed a tiny sigh of relief and opened the first-aid kit. He grabbed a pair of gloves and put them on. He hoped like hell there wouldn't be any complications because he wasn't equipped to handle that and getting Talyssa to the hospital would likely be a fight he'd lose.

Zayne

He kept mostly away from the bedroom, telling himself it was so he wouldn't disturb Nash and Talyssa, but really, he'd never experienced a birth before, and he hadn't been prepared for everything it entailed. He'd seen a lot of shit overseas, but this was a whole other thing. Hearing Talyssa's screams, knowing she was in pain and that there was absolutely nothing he could do about it tore him up inside.

He checked the clock on his phone and grimaced. It'd only been about an hour since Nash arrived, but it felt like much longer. He went to the bedroom and peeked through the door.

"Almost there. You're so close." Nash dried the sweat dripping down his forehead off with his arm. "Next time, give me a big push."

Zayne froze for a moment, for the first time realizing that the baby was actually coming. From the sound of it, that baby would be born any second now. He went to the nursery and grabbed one of the blankets and on his way back, he went to the bathroom to get a towel, too. He knew babies came out slippery and bloody.

He drew in a deep breath, hoping to steady himself before walking into the room. He went to stand by the side of the bed and put the towel next to Nash so he could reach it if necessary. He re-folded the blanket, so it'd hopefully fit around the baby. He didn't know how much time passed but suddenly it was clear that this was it. He kept his eyes on Talyssa's face until he heard the loud wail. He glanced at Nash, then down at the baby in his arms.

"It's a girl," Nash said, wonder in his voice.

Zayne had to pull himself together. He helped Nash get the blanket around the baby and then kept a hand around Nash's upper arm as he stood to hand the baby over to Talyssa.

"You wanna cut the cord?" Nash asked Hawk.

Zayne held back a laugh at the horrified expression on Hawk's face.

"Nic," Talyssa said in a breathy voice. "I just pushed her out of my vagina. Just cut the fucking cord."

Zayne hung back as Hawk unwillingly cut the cord while Nash checked to make sure everything was as it should be with Talyssa. Zayne went to the kitchen and grabbed a few bottles of water from the fridge. He'd only just closed the fridge door when he heard someone enter the room. He turned to see Nash walk toward the table.

"I can't believe I just delivered a baby," Nash said and fell into a chair.

Zayne smiled at him and pushed a water bottle across the table.

"Thanks."

He watched as Nash downed the whole thing. Nash put the empty bottle on the table and dried his mouth off with his arm.

"She's lucky the baby's so small. If she'd been facing the wrong way or if Talyssa had needed to be cut open, we would've had to take them to the hospital, or they could've both died. So much could've gone wrong."

"But it didn't," Zayne said.

"We got lucky," Nash said bobbing his head. He took a deep breath before getting up. "Let's get Nic and Talyssa some of that water. I'm sure they'll need it."

Zayne nodded and let Nash walk ahead of him into the bedroom. He threw one bottle at Hawk, knowing he'd catch it, and handed the other to Talyssa after unscrewing the cap. She let Nash take the baby while she drank. A phone rang, startling both the baby and Talyssa. Hawk cursed under his breath and apologized before pulling his phone out of his pocket. After a few seconds, he put the phone against his chest so whoever was on the other end couldn't hear, and said, "It's Doc."

"Tell him to get his ass back here," Zayne said.

Nic nodded and walked out of the room, probably to threaten the man without Talyssa and Nash overhearing it. The doctor knew better than to leave them waiting.

He felt Nash right next to him and when he turned to him, his eyes landed on the sweet bundle in his arms. He'd never seen a newborn before. She was beautiful and ugly all at the same time and he just knew he'd protect her with his life. He would never let anything happen to her or her mother. He ran his fingertips down her cheek and couldn't help but smile when she blinked her big, blue eyes up at him. She seemed content in Nash's arms and he couldn't blame her.

"Doc will be here tomorrow. I'll stay until he gets here," Hawk said.

"Good," Nash said, turning to smile at Talyssa. "You shouldn't be alone and if you don't feel well or you think there's something wrong with her, you have to go to the hospital."

Hawk opened his mouth to protest but Nash cut him off, saying, "I know they're in danger. Zayne told me. But what's the point in keeping them safe if they end up hurt because of it? Doesn't make sense."

"If anything does happen, Nic will take them to the emergency room," Zayne said, his eyes on Hawk to make sure the man understood that it was an order. Hawk gave a barely visible nod of his head.

Nash sat down next to Talyssa, handing her the baby. "So, with that settled, I've got a question."

Talyssa arched a brow at him.

"Do you know what you're gonna name her?" Nash asked.

"I've known for a while now that I wanted to name her after someone very important to me." Talyssa looked up at Hawk. "Her name's Nicoleta."

Hawk froze, staring at Talyssa with shock in his eyes. Zayne couldn't say he was surprised she'd named the baby after him. Those two had had something special between them from the beginning.

Talyssa stood and placed the baby in Hawk's arms and showed him how to properly hold her. Hawk looked terrified, though Zayne figured that was more because he was afraid to hurt or drop the baby than anything else. The man was looking down at the baby in his arms with so much affection. He'd never seen Hawk as protective as he was of Talyssa and now baby Nicoleta. The Hawk he knew from the club didn't give a shit about anyone.

"Why do I have a feeling that's a rare sight?" Nash asked.

Zayne tore his eyes away from Hawk to look at Nash.

"Nic's not really a people person."

Nash nodded thoughtfully and pulled his phone out of his pocket. Zayne watched him curiously as he took a picture of Hawk and the baby. Nash cocked his head to the side and watched them for a moment before putting his phone away again. When he noticed Zayne's gaze on him, he said, "For Talyssa. I was thinking she might like a picture from today."

"That's…" Zayne shook his head, a smile spreading on his lips. "Very sweet of you. She'll love that."

Nash gave him a shy smile and walked over to Talyssa, probably to show her the pictures. Nash's shirt was a bit bloodied, so Zayne went in search of the clothes he knew Hawk kept at the house. He found a black, long-sleeved shirt that looked like it might fit Nash. He gave it to Nash who thanked him and went to the bathroom to change.

Zayne heated up some food for them all and they ate in the bedroom while Nicoleta slept on her mother's chest. They talked quietly for a while until Talyssa nodded off. Hawk was sitting in the armchair next to Talyssa's bed, his feet up on the bed and his eyes closed. Zayne knew that even if the man was asleep, he was hyperaware and the smallest sound would wake him up, so he let the man sleep.

Nash stood and stretched his arms over his head, a yawn escaping him. A glance out the window made Zayne grimace at the light of day. It had to be in the early morning hour.

"I should get home. I've already given Talyssa my number and told her to call any time," Nash said.

"That's very kind of you. Thank you." Zayne got up. "How did you get here?"

"A friend dropped me off."

"I can give you a lift if you want? Where do you live?" Zayne asked.

"Fell's Point."

Zayne felt a teasing smile form on his lips. "The fancy part of town, huh?"

Nash rolled his eyes, but a chuckle escaped him. "Not always as fancy as it sounds. But it is nicer than the west side."

Zayne grabbed a jacket for Nash on their way through the mudroom. He led Nash to the garage where he handed him the jacket before opening the garage door and walking up to his bike. He grabbed the spare helmet from the saddlebags and turned to hand it to Nash but found the man staring at him with wide eyes, the jacket still in his hands.

"What? Never rode a bike before?"

Nash swallowed and licked his lips before saying, "No."

"Don't worry. You'll like it," Zayne said with an easy smile.

Nash looked uncertain, but he shrugged into the jacket and took the helmet. He didn't seem to need any help getting it on so Zayne just turned to put on his own. Nash gave him his address, then got on the bike behind him and Zayne was smirking as he grabbed Nash's arms, pulling them around his middle.

"Hold on," Zayne said and started the motorcycle.

He drove out of the garage, waiting a few seconds in the driveway to make sure the door closed after them before taking off onto the street. He couldn't help his satisfied smile when Nash's arms tightened around him and he pushed his body against Zayne's back.

The drive took less than fifteen minutes what with it being four in the morning and as time went, he felt Nash relax more behind him. He had a feeling it wouldn't take much to make Nash fall in love with riding. He pulled up in front of Nash's building. He waited for Nash to get off before taking his helmet off. He took Nash's helmet and laid both on the seat after standing.

"Thank you. For the ride," Nash said.

"Anytime." Zayne cocked his head to the side. "You gonna invite me up?"

Nash's eyes went wide, and he opened his mouth, but nothing came out. Nash shook his head and cleared his throat before asking, "Do you want to? Come up, I mean?"

Zayne took a step closer, a smile quirking at his lips when he noticed Nash's breathing becoming labored.

"Did you think I wouldn't want to?"

Nash shook his head. "I wasn't sure. You didn't call and then I figured bikers probably weren't…." Nash licked his lips. "You know…?"

"Gay?"

Nash nodded, his voice breathy as he said, "Yeah. That."

Zayne cocked a brow at him and took a step closer. "I can't be gay if I'm a biker, is that what you think?"

"I don't know what to think."

"Maybe that's the problem," Zayne said. "You're thinking too much."

Before Nash could say anything, Zayne brought their mouths together. Nash's lips were soft and hesitant against his. Zayne cupped Nash's cheeks. Nash opened his mouth for him, and he didn't waste any time shoving his tongue inside. Nash's fingers clutched Zayne's shirt. Their tongues tangled, exploring and savoring. He'd known kissing Nash would be something else, but he hadn't expected it to be mind-blowing.

A phone ringing pulled them apart. Zayne cursed as he got out his phone. With a fleeting glance at Nash, he picked up, barely listening to the voice in his ear. Nash was watching him with dark, hungry eyes.

"I have to go," Zayne said to Nash after hanging up.

The disappointment he saw on Nash's face mirrored how he felt but he wasn't done with Nash. Not in the least. He reached out, cupping Nash's face and kissed him, lingering for a second before pulling back. He took a step back, saying. "You've got my number now. Use it."

Chapter Four

Nash

HE WOKE up to excessive knocking on his front door. With a groan, he sat up in bed. His head was pounding and the light shining through his window because he'd forgotten the blinds last night was hurting his eyes. He threw the blanket to the side and swung his legs over the edge of the bed, glancing down to make sure he was wearing pants. Finding himself wearing a pair of pajama bottoms, he stood and made his way to the door. He unlocked the front door and when he opened it to Harper's smiling face, he groaned loudly.

"How are you awake?" he asked in a groggy voice.

Harper tsked at him and pushed her way past him into the apartment. Mel was there, too. She held up a paper bag with a smile on her lips.

"We figured you might need some breakfast."

He stepped back to let her inside. By the time they reached the kitchen, Harper had already set plates and glasses on the breakfast bar. There were only two bar chairs, so Harper stayed on the other side of the bar, standing up.

"That from Kody's?" Nash asked with a tilt of his head toward the bag.

Mel nodded and pulled a breakfast sandwich out, laying it on his plate. They ate in silence for all of two minutes before Harper couldn't hold back what she'd obviously come there to talk about.

"Caleb said you got a call last night," Harper prompted.

Nash dropped his head back and sighed.

"Yes, I got a call. Yes, Ford gave me a lift, and yes it was a guy."

Harper leaned forward, putting her elbows on the bar and resting her chin in her hands.

"Keep going," she urged.

He shook his head and said, "There's really not much more to say."

"Did he kiss you?" Mel asked, making Nash give her the stink eye.

"Yes."

Harper gasped dramatically, her eyes going wide as she started bouncing.

"Will you please stop? We just kissed. Then he got called away, and that's it."

"He a cop?" Harper asked, raising a brow at him.

Nash refused to answer that. Mostly because he was pretty sure telling Harper who and what Zayne was wouldn't end well and because his silence would make her come to her own conclusion.

"He is, isn't he?" Harper put her elbows on the bar top and leaned toward Nash. "Does he work for BPD or BCPD?"

Nash stood and picked up his and Mel's plates. He walked around the bar, saying, "I'm not telling you anything."

Harper kept trying to get something out of him for the next twenty minutes, but Nash kept his mouth shut, which only made her try harder. When she realized he wasn't going to talk, she sulked for a moment before finding something else to gossip about. She kept talking even as she began washing off their plates.

"Are you gonna see him again?" Mel asked, keeping her voice too low for Harper to hear.

Nash sighed. "I hope so."

Mel nudged his shoulder with hers, making him turn his gaze on her.

"You look happy. I like that look on you."

He glanced down, feeling a smile tease his lips. He was liking it, too.

Zayne

He sat down in one of the couches in the clubhouse with a heavy sigh. He leaned back, rubbing the bridge of his nose.

"Fuck," he breathed.

It'd been too long since he'd slept. After dropping Nash off last night, he'd gone straight back to the clubhouse.

"Long night?" Gabriel asked, sitting down on the couch across from him.

"You could say that."

"Did you guys get anything from the Henchman?"

"How do you know about that?" Zayne asked.

Gabriel hadn't been at the clubhouse when Hawk had shown up with the guy and the other prospects knew to keep their traps shut, even to each other. None of the brothers would've told Gabriel.

"Joker told me."

Zayne arched a brow at him. "Did he now?"

Red tinted Gabriel's cheeks as he glanced down at his hands.

"Well, maybe not entirely intentionally," Gabriel said.

"That so?"

Gabriel shrugged and said, "He came by the house and talked to Pops about it. I just happened to be in the living room with the window open as they walked by outside."

"Yeah, I'm sure you just *happened* to be there," Zayne said.

"It's not like anyone around here tells me anything. I'm the only one who didn't know, aren't I?"

At Zayne's lack of answer, Gabriel scoffed and said, "You guys have to stop treating me like the prez's son and start treating me like any other prospect."

"The only problem with that, kid, is that you aren't just any prospect," Joker said from behind Zayne.

Zayne looked up at Joker, but his eyes were on Gabriel who was squirming under his hard gaze. Gabriel was avoiding Joker's eyes, his jaw clenched. Joker walked around the couch to stand in front of Gabriel. He put two fingers under Gabriel's chin, turning his face up.

"Your father doesn't think you've earned the right to wear our colors and I tend to agree. In my opinion, you don't have what it takes to be a part of this club. Not yet."

Gabriel's face turned red and he pushed Joker's hand away. He stood, forcing Joker to take a step back.

"You can take your opinion and shove it up your ass," Gabriel hissed and stormed off.

Zayne pressed his lips together to keep from smiling. Joker turned to him, a puzzled expression on his face.

"Why does he always get like that with me?" Joker asked.

"You don't see it, do you?"

Joker arched an eyebrow at him. "See what?"

"The kid's in love with you," Zayne said.

Joker's mouth fell open and he stared at Zayne with wide eyes.

"No." Joker shook his head. "He is not in love with me. He's a fucking kid."

"He's twenty-two," Zayne said with a shrug.

"King would kill me."

"Only if you fuck his son."

Joker gave him a dirty look, but Zayne just shrugged. Gabriel had been crushing on Joker for years, but lately, it seemed like it'd become more than a crush. Ever since he'd returned from college and started prospecting, he'd more or less been glued to Joker's side. How Joker didn't see it was a mystery to him.

A glance at his phone showed two messages from Nash. He sent a text back and pushed to his feet.

"Fucking hell," he said as he stretched his arms over his head. "Imma go find myself a bed."

"I'll see you tomorrow, then," Joker said with a knowing gleam in his eyes.

"You know it."

Zayne grabbed his jacket, putting it on as he headed for the door.

Nash

He'd texted Zayne twice. The second time to make sure he'd actually gotten the first one. He tried to convince himself he wasn't being needy, but he was far from succeeding. He'd put his phone, screen down, on the coffee table and turned on the TV. He was watching one of his favorite shows when his phone buzzed. He was almost afraid to check it. He had to read the words twice before the meaning of them finally registered. Zayne was coming over.

"Oh shit," he muttered to himself.

He began pacing his living room, which meant he was only taking four steps, turning, and taking another four steps. He didn't know what to do with himself. He'd wanted Zayne to come over but now that he was on his way, nerves started to kick in. His hands were getting clammy and he didn't know what to do with them. What would Zayne think of his apartment? He should probably tidy it up a bit. Or a lot.

He was washing the last of his dirty dishes when there was a knock on his front door. He dropped the plate he was holding into the sink and tried hard not to run as he made his way to the front door. He yanked open the door and the sight that met him took his breath away. Zayne looked even rougher than he had any of the other times he'd seen him. The stubble on his cheeks made him look sexy as all hell. He blinked up at Zayne, finding the man smiling wryly at him.

"Are you done ogling, or do I need to stay in the doorway longer?"

Nash licked his lips and shook his head. Without a word, he stepped back and held the door open for Zayne who stepped inside. Zayne grabbed the door from him and closed it. Nash cleared his throat.

"Maybe we should—"

He was cut off by Zayne's mouth on his. Zayne walked him backwards until he hit the wall. Zayne moved his lips down Nash's neck.

"Or we can do that," Nash said, his voice breathy.

He closed his eyes and dropped his head back against the wall. Zayne nibbled along his jaw. A groan pushed through his lips when Zayne pressed his thigh between his legs. Desire was spreading through his body like wildfire. His cock was getting harder by the second. He didn't think he'd ever wanted someone as much as he wanted Zayne right then. He wanted to tear off his clothes, get his hands, lips, and teeth on all that delicious skin of Zayne's.

He ran his hands up Zayne's chest, pulling on his leather vest to get it off. Zayne's hand shot out, grabbing Nash's wrist and stopping him. Nash moved his eyes up to meet Zayne's gaze and swallowed hard at the intensity in Zayne's green eyes.

"You should know something," Zayne said, his voice rough and deep.

Nash licked his lips before asking, "What's that?"

"A biker's patches, his cut, it's something he's worked hard to earn. You treat the cut with respect."

Nash nodded but Zayne's fingers tightened around his wrist.

"Will you let me? Please?" Nash asked, staring into Zayne's eyes.

Zayne let go of him, sliding his fingers down Nash's arm and sending a shiver through his body. He slid Zayne's cut slowly off of his shoulders, making sure it didn't fall to the floor. He folded it carefully.

"Where do you want it?"

Zayne took it from him and placed it on the dresser. Then Zayne pulled his shirt over his head, exposing his delicious upper body. Nash was still staring when Zayne put his hands back on him. Nash bit down on his lip, his gaze shooting up to meet Zayne's eyes. Zayne ran his thumb along Nash's lips, pulling his bottom lip free from between his teeth.

"Bedroom?"

Nash didn't answer, he just began pulling Zayne in the right direction. In the bedroom, he led Zayne to his bed and turned them around so Zayne's back was to the bed. He put his hands on Zayne's chest, running them over the hard muscles and swallowed a groan. A grin spread on his lips and he gave Zayne a push, making him sit down on the bed. The heat, the lust, in Zayne's eyes as he looked up at Nash, it was almost too much, too good to be true. He put a knee on either side of Zayne's thighs and settled into Zayne's lap, cupping Zayne's face and leaning down to press their lips together.

Zayne slid his hands down Nash's back to his ass where he grabbed a handful of each cheek. Nash moaned into Zayne's mouth, his hips jerking forward. Zayne's tongue explored his mouth while his hands did wicked things to Nash's body. When they came up for air, Nash was breathing heavily, his eyes on Zayne's.

"I need you out of all these clothes," Zayne said, his voice rough.

Nash's Adam's apple bobbed, and he got to his feet, already pulling at the hem of his shirt. Zayne stood, pushing Nash a few steps back. Nash fumbled with his shirt, unable to get it off while staring at Zayne. Zayne was watching him with hunger in his eyes. He helped Nash get the shirt off and then he ran his hands down Nash's chest, the touch sending sparks of heat through his body. Zayne's fingers found the button on Nash's jeans. Nash held still as Zayne opened his pants. He forgot how to breathe when Zayne pulled his pants down, then kneeled in front of him to get them off and leaned close to press a kiss to Nash's stomach. Zayne looked up at him as he pulled on the waistband of Nash's boxers, moving them down and freeing his rock hard cock. Nash stepped out of his pants.

"Get on the bed," Zayne said, the commanding tone of his voice turning Nash on more than he'd thought it would.

He didn't waste any time getting on the bed. He watched as Zayne got off his knees and undressed, enjoying every second of it. The man was gorgeous. It was clear from the way his body looked that he worked out regularly and took great care of his body. Nash licked his lips when his eyes landed on Zayne's hard and leaking cock.

Now that he was seeing Zayne without clothes on, he noticed the tattoo on his left arm. It was the same skull wearing a crown with a tint of red as on the back of Zayne's cut. Above it was written 'Salvation Kings' in bold letters.

"What do you want, Nash?"

He jerked his eyes up to meet Zayne's inquiring gaze and realized Zayne had moved closer to the bed. Nash rolled to the side, reaching for his nightstand. He pulled out the drawer and reached in to grab a condom and a bottle of lube. He put both on the bed between them and looked up, meeting Zayne's burning gaze.

"You," Nash said and licked his lips nervously. "I want you."

Green eyes locked with his and then the man was on top of him. Zayne thrust against him, rubbing their cocks together and making Nash cry out. His hands went to the back of Zayne's broad shoulders, his fingers digging into the hot skin there.

Zayne's mouth came down on his, Zayne's tongue pushing past his lips and taking control of the kiss. Zayne pulled back, grabbing the lube and squirting some onto his fingers. Nash swallowed hard at the dark look in Zayne's eyes. Zayne ran a hand up Nash's thigh, pushing his legs farther apart. Nash dropped his head back onto the bed, his hands fisting the sheet.

Fingers circled his entrance, teasing for a moment before one pushed inside. He groaned at the burn and stretch, only wanting more. He nearly came off the bed when wet heat surrounded his cock. His eyes shot open. Zayne's lips were wrapped around the head of his cock, his cheeks hollowing as he sucked. Zayne took him to the back of his throat again and again, alternating the speed and driving Nash crazy.

"Fuck," Nash breathed. "So good."

He cried out when a second finger entered him. Nash's legs fell further apart as he panted, his patience close to running out. Zayne swallowed him down, crooking his fingers and hitting the right spot inside Nash. He writhed on the bed, unintelligible sounds coming out of him. Zayne let Nash's cock slip from his lips.

"You wanna come like this?"

"Fuck," Nash said breathlessly. He shook his head. "No. Wanna come with you inside me."

A wicked smile played on Zayne's lips for a second, then he leaned down to lick a path up Nash's cock. Zayne added another finger. Nash's hold on the sheet tightened as his hips bucked up. He was cursing by the time Zayne removed his fingers.

Nash rolled over, getting on his hands and knees. He felt Zayne behind him, a hand sliding up his back. He hissed when the head of Zayne's cock pushed against the tight ring of muscles. He wanted Zayne inside him more than anything right then. Wanted Zayne to fuck him hard and make it so he'd feel it for days.

"You're so fucking sexy like this," Zayne said, his voice thick with lust.

Zayne snapped his hips, driving his cock deep into Nash.

"Holy fuck," Nash gasped.

Zayne's hands slid down his back, the touch scorching hot. Zayne held him by the hips and pulled almost all the way out before pushing back in slowly. Nash whimpered.

"More," Nash panted, barely able to get the word out.

He needed Zayne to move. Zayne seemed to be on the same page because he began thrusting, his pace picking up speed fast. The only sounds in the room were the slapping of skin and Nash's moans. A hand wrapped around his throat, the pressure forcing him upright. Zayne's other hand stayed on Nash's hip, holding him steady. He reached back, grabbing at Zayne's slick skin for purchase. Nash moaned when Zayne thrust into him hard, over and over. He turned his head, seeking out Zayne's mouth. Lips caught his in a rough, desperate kiss.

He moved one hand to wrap his fingers around his cock, pumping his hand in time with Zayne's thrusts. Zayne was hitting his prostate every time. The pressure against his throat grew and he felt his orgasm building fast while Zayne's thrusts grew erratic.

"Zayne," he gasped.

"That's it, baby."

Teeth nibbled at his earlobe, biting down just hard enough to make Nash's eyes roll into the back of his head. Pleasure coursed through his body and he came, spurting all over his hand and the bed. The hand around his throat disappeared, and he fell onto his hands. Zayne pulled out and Nash moaned loudly when he felt Zayne's come hit his back.

He was still trying to catch his breath when lips feathered up his neck, moving to that spot below his ear. A shiver ran through his body.

Zayne moved from behind him, getting off the bed. Nash heard the water turn on in the bathroom. Once his body started to work again, he sat up. He glanced over his shoulder when he heard Zayne walk back into the room. Zayne was carrying a washcloth and he used it to clean up the mess he'd made on Nash. When he was done, he threw it into the laundry basket.

Nash turned around and pushed off the bed. Zayne reached for him, pulling him against his chest. Nash wrapped his arms around Zayne's neck, capturing his lips in a soft kiss. Zayne groaned into his mouth, his hands sliding down Nash's back to grab his ass.

"Let's do that again," Nash said, leaning back in Zayne's arms.

"Liked that, did you?" Zayne asked with a smug smile.

"You know damned well I did."

Chapter Five

Zayne

HIS PHONE buzzing on the nightstand woke him up. He groaned as he reached for it, Nash's arm around his middle preventing him from moving far. When he managed to grab the phone it was to see two missed calls and a text message telling him to pull his head out of his ass and get to the club.

He didn't have time for a shower, but he didn't mind having Nash's smell on him seeing as he might not be back for a while. He grabbed his pants from the floor and pulled them on. He found the rest of his clothes spread around the room and got dressed as quietly as he could. He glanced at Nash lying on the bed, one leg over the blanket and his face buried in a pillow. He bent down to press a kiss to Nash's cheek before walking out of the bedroom and into the hallway where he stopped by the dresser.

He picked up his cut and put it on, his lips twitching into a smile. He hadn't expected Nash to fold it or to even understand just how important his cut was to him. Without it, he was nothing. Without the club, he wasn't even sure he'd be alive.

"Leaving already?"

He turned to find Nash standing in the doorway to his bedroom, a sleepy look on his face. He was only wearing boxer briefs and his bare chest quickly got Zayne's attention. He wanted to lick those abs. Wanted to kiss his way down Nash's chest and hear all those sounds he'd make.

"I have to go. Club business."

Nash arched an eyebrow at him and stepped closer. "It's so important you'd skip out on morning sex?"

A groan pushed past Zayne's lips. The teasing smile on Nash's face made him cross the hallway and pull Nash into his arms. He crushed his mouth over Nash's and slid a hand to the back of Nash's neck. Nash opened his mouth to him with a low moan and he slipped his tongue inside. The kiss got heady fast. He pulled back, unwillingly, knowing he had to get going if he wanted to avoid an ass whooping.

"Fuck," he breathed.

"We could," Nash said with a hopeful smile.

Zayne took a step back, shaking his head at Nash.

"I can probably be back in a few hours if you don't have to work?"

A smile widened Nash's lips.

"I don't have to work until Tuesday."

Zayne arched a brow at him. "Really?"

"We have four days on, four days off." Nash shrugged. "I don't have any plans the next two days. Not unless you wanna make some?"

Zayne cupped Nash's cheeks and stepped closer. "Oh, I do."

He brought their lips together in a quick kiss. Nash was wearing a shy smile when he stepped back.

"I'll call you when I know what time I'll be back," Zayne said.

"Okay."

Zayne had to pull himself away or he would just keep kissing Nash and then he wouldn't be going anywhere for a while. He shoved his hands into his pockets and backed away. Nash watched him with a knowing smile on his lips until he reached the front door. He turned and opened the door, taking a step out before stopping to look over his shoulder. Nash was still standing there, his eyes on Zayne's ass. Zayne shook his head, a chuckle escaping him. Nash's gaze shot up to his and Nash gave him an unapologetic smile.

Zayne walked out the door knowing he'd much rather stay. As he walked from Nash's building to his bike, something made him stop and look around. He didn't see anything out of place but the hair rising at the back of his neck told him something was off. With another glance around as he continued to his bike, he decided he was being paranoid. He didn't see anything or anyone suspicious.

He unlocked his saddlebag and pulled out his helmet. With the helmet on, he got on the bike and took off onto the street. He drove to the club and tried to shake the feeling of being watched. He parked his bike next to King's and took off his helmet. He noticed Viper's bike and frowned. As far as he knew, Viper was supposed to be in York, keeping an eye on the Henchmen. As he walked toward the door to the clubhouse, Joker stepped outside.

"What's so important I had to skip morning sex?"

That got an actual smile on Joker's face. A rather terrifying one, but still a smile.

"The paramedic?" Joker asked.

Zayne nodded and said, "Yep."

He was probably smiling like a lunatic. He hadn't felt this great in a long time.

"Good for you, brother," Joker said and gave him a friendly slap on the back.

"Really, though. Why am I here?"

"We've got a new shipment."

Zayne felt a frown form on his forehead. "Already?"

"Yeah. They're all level five, too," Joker said. "All seven of them."

"Shit."

Their supplier had a very complex system and a level five was as bad and as dangerous as it got. Usually, they left those to the enforcers because they were better equipped to handle them. But level fives also usually only came in ones or twos. They'd never done seven at once before.

Auggie stuck his head out the door and yelled, "Church. Now."

They followed Auggie inside to the room they used for Church. Church was only for patched-in members, so he was surprised to see Gabriel there. Zayne sat down in his designated chair next to Joker.

"What's he doing here?" Joker asked with a nod toward Gabriel.

King sighed and said, "He's here because we need him for this. We're eight men down right now and we've got seven level fives on our hands. Two of them are kids and we all know how easily they get scared of us. Especially with what these two have been through. So, that's where Gabe comes in."

"For once, I don't mind being the least scary here," Gabriel said.

"One is going to New Jersey. One to Pittsburg. The three others are going to Chicago. Emanuel will take them from there, but we can't risk transporting them all together. Too many people after them," King said and began dividing them into teams.

They were always two to three people on every delivery. It was safest that way. Not too many to draw attention but enough to ensure the safety of the people they were transporting. Under normal circumstances, they'd keep them at the club for a day or two to let things settle down. But from what King was telling them, they wouldn't have time for that. They'd already arrived, and they needed to be delivered as fast as possible.

"Joker. Saint. You're with Gabe and the kids," King said.

King handed Gabriel a burner phone and Zayne pushed out of his chair. He glanced down at Joker when he remained seated and found his friend brooding. He fought a smile and cleared his throat to get Joker's attention. Joker stood, annoyance plastered all over his face as he walked past Zayne.

"This is gonna be a fucking shit show," Joker grumbled.

Nash

He was sitting on a bench at the Inner Harbor, looking out over the water and enjoying the light breeze. When Zayne had texted to let him know he wouldn't be back until tomorrow, he hadn't been sure if he was getting the brush-off or if it was really the truth, but then he'd gotten a call from Zayne. That deep, husky voice in his ear caused shivers to run down his spine and got his pulse spiking. Zayne telling him how much he wanted to be back in his bed, wanted to touch and kiss him, made him wish Zayne could get back faster.

Someone sat down next to him with a loud huff.

"Why does it have to be so hot?"

He glanced over at his best friend, Alanna, who was fanning herself with a leaflet. She looked at him with her beautiful hazel eyes and thrust her lip out in a pout. The weather was a bit crazy. The heat had spiked over the past few days.

"Hello to you, too. How's your boy toy doing?" he asked with a teasing smile.

"Still healing and still afraid my father will smother him in his sleep."

"Poor Brent," Nash said. He meant it too. Dating a police captain's daughter was one thing but working for that same captain while secretly having dated his daughter for months, that was a whole other thing. Brent was lucky to be alive and not because he'd been shot on the job.

"Is he walking?" Nash asked.

Alanna nodded and said, "A bit. Which is very good. The doctors weren't sure he'd ever walk again."

"God. Could you imagine if he was stuck in a wheelchair and couldn't be a cop anymore?"

"I would've killed his grumpy ass by now," Alanna said.

He could believe that. Brent lived for his job. Even on his days off, he was itching to get back. He wasn't much different in that aspect to Alanna's father.

"How's your dad?"

"Still pissed I screwed one of his detectives and didn't tell him."

Nash burst into laughter and said, "I can imagine."

Alanna's father was a big man and not just in height and width. He'd chased off many boys when they'd been in high school. He wasn't shy about showing off his huge collection of pistols, rifles, and machine guns.

"Enough about me. What's going on with you?"

"What do you mean?" Nash asked and glanced down at his hands.

"Aha. That right there is all I needed. Did you get your hands on a sexy hunk without telling me?"

Nash shushed her and glanced around, but, thankfully, no one was paying them any attention. It wasn't that long since he'd officially come out and Baltimore wasn't exactly that LGBT friendly a place.

"Alright. Yeah. We met through work," Nash said.

Alanna looked like she wanted to grill him for information, but she wasn't his best friend for nothing. She knew him well enough to know he'd tell her when he was ready.

A beep made him glance down at the round, black device lying between them. A small light was flashing on it.

"Our table's ready," he said and stood, waiting for Alanna to follow suit.

They walked into the restaurant where they were led to a table with a nice view of the harbor. While they waited for their food, Alanna told him about the place her sister was considering renting for her auto shop and he just sat back and listened to her talk, loving the pride that shone through in her voice.

Zayne

Gabriel's burner phone had the address they'd be dropping the kids off at. Fortunately, it wasn't too far. A three hour's drive each way. If he was lucky, he'd be back in time to see Nash that night, but he'd told him he probably wouldn't be back until the next day just in case.

Usually, he was the one who planned any and all trips they went on because he was the road captain, but whenever they got one of these jobs it was always with specific and pre-planned locations. It was a decent-paying job but that wasn't why any of them were in it. When King had been approached about it, he'd put it to a vote, and it'd been a unanimous yay. Helping people in need was pretty much a cornerstone in their club. They didn't have salvation in their name for nothing.

"I have to pee."

Zayne turned in his seat to look at the little girl on a car-seat behind him. She was looking up at him with her big brown eyes.

"We're almost there, sweetie," Gabriel said. He was sitting on the backseat behind Joker with Emma between him and Miles.

The kids had been easy so far, though he didn't think they'd ever had so many pee and food breaks on a three-hour drive before. Emma was five and her brother was seven. They were both much more adjusted than he'd expected two kids who'd lost their parents and then been forced to flee across the country could be. Either their parents had done one hell of a job raising them, or they'd just been born that way.

They'd taken to Gabriel like King had suspected they would, but at their first stop, Emma had taken Zayne's hand and ordered him to accompany her to the restroom. She'd refused to use any other bathroom than the women's and then she'd looked at him with her big puppy eyes and he'd had no choice but to go with her. He'd stayed by the sinks, receiving a whole lot of stink eye from the women there until Emma came out to wash her hands.

"Fifteen minutes," Joker said.

"You think you can wait that long?" Zayne asked Emma.

She sighed, crossed her arms and leaned back in her seat.

"I don't like it, but for you, I'll hold it," she said.

Zayne caught Gabriel's gaze and it was all he could do to hold back a laugh. She was something else, that sweet girl.

When Joker finally pulled into the parking lot of a seedy-looking motel, Emma was half asleep. Zayne glanced around, looking for anyone lurking in the shadows. There weren't anyone outside, so he opened his car door and got out. He caught Joker's gaze across the top of the car.

"I'll get a room," Joker said and walked off.

Gabriel stepped out on the other side while Zayne opened the door for Emma and helped her out.

"Alright. Let's get your stuff," Gabriel said to the kids.

Zayne popped the trunk and grabbed the small, purple backpack first. He handed it to Emma who'd insisted from the start that she could carry her own things. He didn't mind her carrying her backpack, but he wasn't about to let her carry the duffle bag with her clothes and other stuff in it.

They waited for Joker to return with a room key and when he did, he led them to their room. Joker opened the door and walked inside. Emma followed him, bouncing on her toes, so Zayne showed her to the bathroom. Joker sat down in the only chair and toed off his boots. Zayne put Emma's bag on the floor by the queen-sized bed. He glanced over his shoulder to see Miles and Gabriel stepping into the room.

"You wanna see something on the TV?" Zayne asked Emma who was now crawling onto the bed.

She nodded so he grabbed the remote. He went through the channels until it landed on one Emma liked. It didn't take long before she was completely immersed in the kid's show. Miles, on the other hand, wasn't so easily distracted. The boy was walking around the room, looking through everything.

"What's that?" Miles asked, making Zayne glance his way.

Miles was standing next to Joker, pointing at the gun showing at Joker's side.

"Something you're not allowed to touch," Joker said with a growl in his voice.

Miles jerked away, a terrified expression on his face. Gabriel laid a hand on his shoulder and guided him toward the bed.

"He's scary," Miles said in a whisper and pointed at Joker.

"You should see him when he smiles," Zayne said.

Gabriel was wearing a displeased look on his face as he glared at Zayne. Zayne shrugged and raised a brow at him.

"What he means is that Joker only looks scary on the outside, but on the inside, he's just a squishy, loving teddy bear," Gabriel said to Miles.

Zayne nearly choked trying to hold back his laughter. A teddy bear was the last thing he'd describe Joker as. From the evil glare Joker was sending Gabriel, he knew if the kids hadn't been there, Gabriel would have been in trouble.

The kids fell asleep fast. They couldn't do anything but wait for their contact to show up. Gabriel was watching the kids while Joker leaned back in his chair, put his feet up on Emma's bag, and closed his eyes. Zayne glanced at his watch. He began pacing, alternating between looking at the kids and checking the clock.

"You got somewhere to be?" Gabriel asked.

Zayne stopped pacing long enough to give Gabriel an unimpressed look.

"He's got a hot piece of ass waiting for him at home. Lucky bastard," Joker said without opening his eyes.

The glare he'd just given Gabriel had nothing on the one Gabriel sent Joker's way. "I need some air," Gabriel said and rushed toward the door.

Zayne kept his eyes on Joker, but the idiot just stayed seated, not at all realizing he'd just upset Gabriel. He really was oblivious. Zayne shook his head at him and grabbed a keycard before following after Gabriel. He found him just outside, his back against the wall and a cigarette between his lips. When Gabriel looked at him, he raised a brow and crossed his arms over his chest.

"Your father know you're smoking?"

Gabriel shook his head and took a drag of the cigarette before saying, "I only smoke when I drink or when I'm stressed."

"And when you're hurt or pissed off?" Zayne guessed.

Gabriel clenched his jaw. "Spare me the speech. I already know I'm being stupid," Gabriel said.

"Gabe." Zayne put a hand on his shoulder. "Joker's the one who's an idiot."

"Then you're the only one who thinks so."

Zayne shrugged and said, "I'm also his best friend and the one who knows him the best."

"My dad would kill him. Even then, he's the VP and he'd never do anything to jeopardize that," Gabriel said, a sad smile on his lips.

Zayne nudged Gabriel's shoulder with his own.

"If he doesn't have the balls to stand up to your dad, then he doesn't deserve you."

Gabriel moved his head in what Zayne assumed was a nod.

"Wouldn't make me want him any less." Gabriel sighed and dropped the cigarette on the ground. "Which is stupid. He doesn't respect me, and he certainly doesn't see me as a man."

"He doesn't respect anyone who can't kick his ass."

Gabriel looked at him with surprise in his eyes. "You've kicked his ass?"

"A time or two."

"I'd love to see that."

"I'm sure you would," Zayne said, a sly smile on his lips. He glanced to his right, noticing someone walking toward them. "We've got company."

Gabriel straightened and turned to look in the same direction as Zayne. The man wore dark sunglasses and a gray cap. When they worked with new people or just people they didn't know, both parties got a codeword to ensure they were meeting the right person.

"Sombrero."

Zayne breathed a sigh of relief and said, "Irish jig."

"Gentlemen. I understand you've got something for me," the man said.

"Two precious packages," Gabriel said with a nod.

"Joker? It's time," Zayne called out as he opened the door.

Joker was helping Emma put her shoes back on when they walked into the room. Miles already had on his shoes and backpack. Zayne walked to the bed and grabbed Emma's bag, slinging it over his shoulder. Once Emma was ready, Joker stood, and Emma slid down the bed to take Zayne's hand. He smiled down at her, sad to see her go but also thrilled that she was about to start her new life. A better and safer one.

They all walked to a minivan parked close to their room and when Zayne went to put Emma's bag in the trunk, Emma kept a hold of his other hand. Miles took off his backpack and handed it to Zayne. When all their things were in the trunk, he closed it.

"He seems sad," Emma said, her gaze on Joker. "He needs someone to make it better. Can you help him?"

Zayne smiled down at her. "I think he needs someone too, sweetie. But he's a big boy. He'll figure it out."

"Hmm. Okay."

Zayne crouched down. Emma wrapped her arms around him and hugged him tightly.

"I'll miss you," she whispered against his chest.

He squeezed her just a bit tighter as he said, "I'll miss you, too."

He let her go and helped her get into the van. There was already a car seat there so when she was seated, he made sure to buckle her in. They said their goodbyes and then Zayne shut the door and stepped back. They watched as the car turned onto the road and drove away. He knew not to get attached but those two had definitely left an impression on him. From the look on Gabriel's face, he felt the same way.

"I'll umm… Go get us checked out," Gabriel said, his eyes on the ground as he turned away from them.

He watched Joker watch Gabriel walk away. The look on Joker's face was one of puzzlement. Perhaps his friend finally noticed Gabriel's dejection.

"Those are some great kids," Zayne said and shook his head. "It's crazy to think that someone wants to hurt them."

"I hear you, brother," Joker said.

"Emma said she thinks you're sad and need someone to make it better. I agree," Zayne said, wagging his eyebrows.

"So, I need to get laid is what you're saying?"

"Pretty much."

But regularly. With the same person. He didn't say that, though. He knew Joker wasn't ready to hear it, let alone do it.

Joker laid a hand on Zayne's shoulder and squeezed.

"Let's go home."

Nash

He put a bowl of ice cream on the coffee table in front of Alanna who immediately reached for it. He sat down next to her with his own bowl in his lap. He didn't like ice cream that much, but he always kept some in the freezer for Alanna.

"So this guy," Alanna prompted, pointing her spoon at him.

Nash groaned. "This again?"

Alanna ignored him in favor of asking, "Is it serious?"

"I think so," Nash said with a bob of his head.

"You *think* so?"

Nash shoved a big spoonful of ice cream into his mouth to keep from answering. Alanna watched him, her eyes narrowed and the expression on her face telling him she wasn't about to let it go. She didn't often push him for answers, so he knew she was deadly serious and probably a little worried.

"You haven't been on a single date with him, have you?"

Nash dropped his head into his hands with a deep sigh.

"No," he mumbled against his palms.

"So it's just sex, but you think it might be serious?"

He removed his hands and sighed, placing his bowl on the table. "I… Look, it's a bit complicated. He's been called away for work twice while he was here, so we haven't really had much time to *discuss* things," Nash said.

"Next time you see him, make sure you talk things through. The last thing I want is for you to end up with a broken heart," she said.

"I will," he promised.

Alanna nodded, seeming satisfied with his answer. She leaned back and put on a movie. Nash put his feet up on the coffee table and Alanna took up the rest of the couch, laying her legs over Nash's lap. They were halfway through the movie when someone knocked on his front door.

"You expecting someone?" Alanna asked with a raised brow.

Nash shook his head and when Alanna moved her legs, he stood. Alanna grabbed the remote and paused the movie, looking up at him with curious eyes. Nash walked into the hallway and to the door. He'd only just pulled the door open when he was attacked. Hands wrapped around his forearms and pulled him against a hard body. Lips crashed over his mouth as he was backed into the wall. He heard something hit the floor and the door slam but all he could think about was Zayne against him, Zayne's lips on his. He slid his fingers into Zayne's hair, their tongues tangling, tasting and exploring.

Zayne broke the kiss and it took Nash a few seconds to find out why. He followed Zayne's line of sight and cringed when he saw Alanna with a shoulder leaned against the doorway as she watched them with a sly smile.

"Oh, don't mind me. Please do continue," Alanna said.

"Who is she and can she leave?" Zayne asked.

Alanna propped a hand on her hip and said, "I'm Alanna. His best friend."

Nash bit his lip against a smile as he shared a look with Alanna. Alanna ran her eyes over Zayne and with a wry smile on her lips, she said, "I approve."

Zayne turned to Nash, his brows drawing together. "I need approving?"

"It's the best friend pact," Alanna said, a serious look in her eyes. "What kind of friend would I be if I didn't vet his boyfriends?"

"Boyfriend?" Zayne asked, his eyebrow raised at Nash.

Nash pressed his lips together. They hadn't even talked about what they were and there Alanna was, saying things like that. He needed her gone before she scared off Zayne.

"Doesn't your boyfriend need a diaper change or something?" Nash asked Alanna.

Alanna burst into laughter and shook her head at him. "I'm gonna tell him you said that." She disappeared into the living room only to reappear with her handbag slung over her shoulder and her phone in hand. She walked past them and winked at Nash.

"Love you. Have fun."

Nash shook his head, a smile teasing his lips as his eyes followed her. The second the door closed behind Alanna, Zayne's lips were back on his. Zayne's hands grabbed at him, pulling him closer. Zayne moved his lips to Nash's neck, kissing and nibbling. Nash groaned and tilted his head to the side to give Zayne better access.

"I missed you," Zayne said against his neck.

Nash shivered when Zayne's lips found that spot beneath his ear. His fingers slid into Zayne's hair, holding on as he moved his lips to Nash's mouth. The kiss was electric, sending sparks of desire through him. They were both gasping for breath when Zayne pulled back. Nash ran his eyes over Zayne's handsome face and down his drool-worthy chest. The t-shirt he was wearing left little to the imagination.

"You're not wearing your cut," Nash said, cocking his head to the side as he watched Zayne with confusion.

Zayne shook his head. "I figured I shouldn't wear it around here seeing as I kinda want to come back as often as possible."

Nash's eyebrows shot up and he blinked at Zayne.

"Really?" he mumbled and cleared his throat. "You want that?"

Zayne nodded, a coy smile on his lips. "If you want it, too?"

He didn't answer, he just crushed his mouth over Zayne's.

Chapter Six

Zayne

WAKING UP next to Nash was something he'd wanted for a long time. He'd known for a while that he was ready to find someone to settle down with, but he hadn't realized how much he'd *needed* it. He went in search of his duffle bag and found it in the hallway where he'd dropped it last night. He'd made sure to have clothes with him so he wouldn't have to go home or to the club to change.

He heard the shower turn on and made his way to the bathroom. Nash was standing by the shower without clothes on, reaching in to check the temperature of the water. Zayne couldn't help himself. He stepped into the bathroom and walked up behind Nash, putting a hand on his hip and pressing his lips to the side of Nash's neck.

"Good morning," Zayne mumbled.

"It is now," Nash said and turned in his arms.

Nash was grinning as he wagged his eyebrows. Zayne shook his head at him but lowered his head to brush his lips over Nash's. Nash leaned into him, running his hands over Zayne's chest. There was no way they could both fit in the shower, so Zayne stepped back and let Nash go first. They both took quick showers and got dressed.

Nash was making them breakfast while Zayne checked in with King. The kids were off to start their new lives with their fake identities and no one hunting them. The Kings were spread thin with so many level fives. Especially with three of them going to Chicago separately. But he'd managed to convince King that he wasn't needed at the clubhouse until the next day.

He walked into the kitchen to see Nash take two bagels from the toaster and put them onto plates. Nash looked up when he heard him and flashed a smile.

"Are you gonna disappear on me today, too?"

Zayne felt his lips quirk and reached out to tug Nash closer. He cupped Nash's face, rubbing his thumbs across his cheeks.

"I'm all yours today," Zayne said.

The smile Nash gave him was breathtaking. He took the plates from Nash and carried them into the living room where they sat down on the couch. They ate in comfortable silence and when they were done, he helped Nash clean up. They were standing in the kitchen, Nash by the sink and Zayne next to him, leaning a hip against the counter. He dried off the last knife Nash had washed and was putting it down when Nash turned to him.

"I think we should talk," Nash said, worrying his bottom lip. "What are we doing?"

There was a joke on the tip of his tongue, but he kept quiet when he noticed how serious Nash seemed.

"What do you mean?"

Nash let out a shaky breath. "Are we just having sex? Are we dating? Are we a thing? Or not a thing at all?"

"Oh, we're definitely a thing," Zayne said. He took a step closer to Nash. "There's something about you, Nash. We have a connection I don't think I've ever had with anyone else before. I would like to explore it with you if that's what you want?"

"Yes," Nash blurted out. He shook his head, a sheepish look on his face. "Yes. I would like that very much."

"I'd better do this right, then," Zayne said.

Nash's confused expression was adorable.

"Will you go on a date with me?" Zayne asked.

Nash nodded eagerly. "Yes. I'd love that."

"Where do you wanna go, then?"

"There's a restaurant downtown. They have amazing Italian food, if you like that?"

"Sure," Zayne said.

"One thing, though," Nash said.

"What's that?"

"There'll probably be a few cops and firefighters there."

"Well, it's a good thing I'm not scared of cops," Zayne said with an easy smile.

He wouldn't be wearing his cut, so he didn't see any problem in going there.

"So, um. Lunch or dinner?"

Zayne gave it some thought before saying, "Dinner. I was thinking, if you want, we could go see how Talyssa and the baby are doing and then get some lunch. Maybe take a walk in Druid Hill Park. What do you say?"

Nash was wearing a wide smile as he said, "I love babies."

Nash

He was very much looking forward to seeing Talyssa again. The baby, too. He'd always loved babies. When Zayne pulled into the garage, he could barely wait to get off the bike. Zayne led the way up the front steps where he pulled out a key and unlocked the door. They stepped inside and were taking off their shoes when Talyssa walked into the hallway.

"Hey," Zayne said in a low voice. "I didn't want to knock in case she was asleep."

"Thank you. Come on in, guys."

They followed her to the living room where a little crib was set up next to an armchair. Talyssa sank into the chair with a sigh. Nash sat down on the couch, pleasantly surprised when Zayne sat down right next to him and put an arm around him.

"Have you had any problems?" Nash asked.

Talyssa waved him off, a smile on her lips as she said, "Don't worry about me. The doctor has already checked me over several times."

Nash opened his mouth but was cut off by a cry. Talyssa reached into the crib to pick up her daughter. Talyssa held Nicoleta against her chest and rocked her and it didn't take long to soothe her.

"You wanna hold her?" Talyssa asked Nash.

Talyssa put the baby in his arms before he could say anything. He smiled down at Nicoleta and found himself completely transfixed by her beautiful blue eyes. She wrapped her tiny fingers around one of his, holding on tightly. He talked to her and told her how beautiful she was until she fell asleep again. He got up to put Nicoleta back into her crib. He laid her down and covered her with the blanket. As he looked at her, he remembered what Zayne had told him about her father the day she was born. *How could anyone ever want to hurt a baby?*

"Some people are monsters," Zayne said.

Nash jerked his head up to look at Zayne, realizing he'd said it out loud. He shifted from one foot to the other and rubbed his neck, his gaze shifting to Talyssa.

"It's alright," Talyssa said and pointed at the couch next to her. "Sit down and why don't I tell you?"

Nash walked around the coffee table and sat down. His eyes were on Talyssa as she spoke.

"My husband is the CEO of a big tech company and he's got a lot of friends in high places. Eight months ago, I found out he was cheating on me, so I asked for a divorce. He didn't take it very well," Talyssa said and looked down at her hands.

"Did he hurt you?" Nash asked, fearing her answer.

Talyssa shook her head and sighed. "No. I almost wish he had. He just yelled and threw things around. I called the cops, but they wouldn't do anything. He hadn't hurt or threatened me."

"That must've been terrifying."

Talyssa nodded. "It was. It also made me open my eyes to what kind of man he really is. I spent another month with him and all of that time I just had this eerie feeling he was planning something bad. By accident, I found out he'd not only taken out a life insurance on me, but he'd increased it after I'd asked for a divorce. I couldn't prove anything, but I knew... I knew he wanted me dead.

"I tried to leave but he stopped me. We'd been trying for a baby for over a year and he'd convinced me to quit my job so I wouldn't be stressed out and then when I did get pregnant, I could be a stay at home mom. Most of my family is gone and without a job, I didn't know where to go. I couldn't provide for myself and then, on top of that, I found out that I was pregnant. That's also when I knew I needed to get away from him, no matter what it took. I began looking for a lawyer who could take my case pro-bono," Talyssa said and shared a smile with Zayne

"And that is how she met Milo, the club's lawyer," Zayne said. "He listened to her story and then he went straight to King."

"They've been protecting and taking care of me ever since," Talyssa said.

"It's not the first time Milo has gotten a client who needed a different kind of help than he could offer them, but I don't think we've tried anything quite like this before."

"That's me," Talyssa said with a sigh. "A one of a kind pain in the ass."

"Awe come on. I doubt anyone would think you're a pain," Nash said.

Talyssa shook her head, a smile teasing her lips.

"Milo told me not to leave his office so I sat there and waited over an hour, thinking my life was over, that he was trying to find a way to help me but couldn't. Then Nic showed up, wearing his leather cut and looking rough as hell. I should've been frightened of him but one look into those sapphire blues and I knew; there was the man who was going to save me."

Zayne leaned forward and said, "No matter how many times I hear you say that, I don't get how you saw him like that. That's not the Nic I know."

"How do you see him, then?" Nash asked, curious to know more about the man.

"He's an enforcer for the club. He's a dangerous man. Not someone most people would see as a protector."

Talyssa shrugged and stood, throwing a glance into Nicoleta's crib before meeting Zayne's gaze.

"Well, he's my hero," she said and walked into the kitchen.

Nash followed her with his eyes until she disappeared. He turned to Zayne, finding the man watching him.

"Do you think those two…?"

Zayne shook his head and said, "I think she's more like a sister to him."

Nash nodded to himself and moved closer to Zayne so he could lean against him. Zayne laid a hand on his thigh and when Nash looked up at him, Zayne placed a kiss to his lips.

They stayed at Talyssa's for another hour before Zayne dragged him away. His stomach rumbled when they walked outside, and he had to admit that he was getting hungry. He got behind Zayne on the bike. He wrapped his arms around Zayne and closed his eyes, enjoying the ride. They went to a deli where they each got a sandwich and a soda, then they drove to the park. They'd decided to find a spot there to sit down and eat. Zayne found a place to park and then they made their way to one of the lakes. He was surprised when Zayne took his hand. He looked up to see Zayne with a relaxed expression on his face. He could definitely get used to that.

Zayne

The restaurant Nash took him to was named Tesoro and he'd never been there before, though he was sure he'd heard one of the women at the club mention it. As they stepped inside, he noticed that it was bigger than it looked from the outside. The atmosphere was calm and welcoming. He immediately liked it.

A waitress walked up to them, smiling wide when she saw Nash.

"Hi, Gemma," Nash said.

"Hi, sweetie. It's been a while, huh? How are you?"

"I'm good," Nash said and glanced at Zayne. "Great, actually."

Gemma looked Zayne up and down. "Mhmm. I can believe that."

"Yeah, um, Gemma this is Zayne," Nash said.

"Nice to meet you, Zayne. C'mon, I'll find you a good table," Gemma said and turned around.

She seated them at a small, intimate table and handed them their menu cards. They placed their order and it wasn't long before Gemma came back with their drinks. Zayne took a sip of his beer and moaned happily.

"So," Nash said.

Zayne leaned back in his seat and raised a brow at him. "So?"

"Where are you from?"

"I was born here but moved around a bit in my teenage years. Then I joined the Army and when I got back, I wanted to be somewhere familiar, so I came here," Zayne said.

"You were in the Army? How did I not know that?" Nash mused.

"I served two tours," Zayne said with pride.

"Really?"

"Yeah. I enlisted along with my best friend and we were lucky enough to end up in the same squad both times. I don't know what I would've done without him over there," Zayne said.

"He means a lot to you, huh?"

Zayne nodded, getting a lump in his throat for a moment. "Yeah. He's like a brother to me. When I asked him to join the club with me, he didn't hesitate."

"How did you go from the Army to a motorcycle club?" Nash asked, nothing but curiosity on his face.

Zayne took a deep breath, letting it out slowly. "When you get home from something like that, you often find that what you once considered home, isn't the same anymore. Nothing's really the same. It's hard to adapt and find your place in the world again. People judge much more than you would think. Except for the club. There's no judging there. No one way to do things."

"Sounds like you found your home again," Nash said.

Zayne nodded. Most people didn't understand the allure of a motorcycle club. Once they saw the one percenter's patch, they decided what and who you were. But the club offered men and women like him a second chance at life. A chance the system couldn't.

Carrying a gun, taking or giving orders, protecting people, and having a brotherhood: a family. That's what it was about for him and for the majority of his brothers and sisters. Sure, there were clubs that dealt in drugs, guns, and prostitution, but his club wasn't like that. They wore the one percenter's patch proudly because it meant they didn't conform to society. Society had let them down again and again. It wasn't strong enough to help them, so they'd become stronger and now they helped others. He was proud to call himself a King.

Gemma came back with their dinner and they dug right in. They were halfway through their meals when Zayne asked, "What about you? Have you always lived in Baltimore?"

"I've never ventured further than Baltimore County."

Zayne put down his cutlery and stared at Nash. "You've never been to any other city?"

"No," Nash said with a shake of his head.

"I think I see a road trip in your future," Zayne said.

"Is that so?"

Zayne hummed affirmatively. He wanted Nash on the back of his bike, and he wanted to take him places he hadn't been before. He wanted to show him so many things.

"But we've gotta get you in shape first," Zayne said.

Nash coughed, almost choking on his food. "I need to what now?"

Zayne looked at him with a playful grin.

"Get in better shape. Riding a bike for that long takes a toll and I only just popped your cherry a few days ago."

Right then, Gemma walked by with a tray of food and she nearly dropped it when she overheard him.

Nash snorted out a laugh and said, "That's what you get for eavesdropping."

Gemma moved the tray to one side so she could flip him off, making Nash laugh. Zayne watched him with an adoring smile.

"So. Do you want to?" Zayne asked.

Nash's smile sent his pulse soaring and he felt relief when Nash nodded.

"Hell yeah," Nash said.

Zayne reached across the table to lay his hand over Nash's.

"You're okay with this?" Nash asked, squeezing his fingers.

Zayne smiled at him and said, "If someone has something to say to me, they can go right ahead. They just won't be able to say another fucked-up thing again."

"Your club is okay with it, too?"

"My prez's son is gay. They've known since he was like four or five and he's twenty-two now, so when King started the club, he decided that we would be completely inclusive. It doesn't matter which gender, sexuality, race, or religion you have as long as you live by the bylaws and honor the colors."

Nash was watching him intensely. There was no judgment in those deep brown eyes. He didn't know how Nash would take actually being at the club and meeting everyone, how he'd do being a part of the club, but he knew he wanted to give it a shot. There was something about the man in front of him. He'd noticed it when they'd first met, too. It was why he'd let him through the gate. It was the compassion he showed, the way Nash looked at people with no preconceived notion. He hadn't experienced that from people very often and even though he knew it might be a risk, he wanted Nash in his life.

Chapter Seven

Nash

IT'D BEEN two weeks since their dinner date at Tesoro and that time had been filled with fun days, scorching nights, and several amazing dates. They'd been out riding on Zayne's motorcycle a few times and each time, he enjoyed it more than the last. Now, he was standing outside his apartment building, wearing a backpack and trying to convince himself they weren't crazy.

"Are we really doing this?" he asked with a glance at Zayne's bike.

Zayne grinned at him and nodded. "We are."

He took the helmet Zayne handed him and put it on. With a last skeptical look at Zayne, he waited for him to get on the bike before sliding on behind him. He wrapped his arms around Zayne's waist and leaned his head against the back of his shoulder.

"D.C. here we come," Zayne said and then they were off.

The first time Zayne had taken him out on a longer ride, he'd brought some of his old riding leathers for Nash to wear. He'd felt like an idiot in all that leather. Of course, Zayne managed to look sexy in his. Then Zayne had growled that he liked seeing Nash wearing his clothes and their ride had been delayed by a few hours.

He was way too excited and nervous about going out of town to even think about what he was wearing. Traffic wasn't all that bad, so they made the trip in a little over an hour. They were going to stay one night so they could get the most out of the trip. They'd be staying with Zayne's sister, Emery, and while he thought it might be a little early to be meeting family members, he was also looking forward to meeting someone important to Zayne.

Zayne found a parking spot in front of Emery's building. They got off the bike and Zayne emptied the saddlebags, handing half the items to Nash. Then Zayne took his hand and tugged him along. They entered the building and walked up the stairs to the second floor where Zayne led them to the first door to the left. Zayne put down his bags and searched through his pockets until he found the key. He unlocked the door while Nash watched, his bottom lip between his teeth. Zayne opened the door and waved Nash inside.

"Em won't be home until after five," Zayne said and put his bag on the floor.

"Oh, okay," Nash said, breathing what he hoped was a silent sigh of relief.

Zayne cocked his brow at him and with a teasing smile on his lips, he asked, "Are you nervous?"

Nash shrugged and turned away from him. Zayne wasn't having it, though. He grabbed Nash's arm, turning him back around and cupped his face.

"You've got nothing to be nervous about," Zayne said. "Em is gonna love you."

"You can't know that."

"I know my sister and I know you."

Nash let out a breath and shook his head. He followed Zayne into the room they'd be sleeping in and they left their bags there after changing out of their riding clothes and into something more casual. After a quick tour of the apartment, they grabbed what they'd need for the day and left. The apartment was only a twenty-minute walk from the capitol, so they started there.

It was a grand building and the staircases were huge. It was strange to think Zayne's sister worked there. They weren't there for long before Zayne took his hand and led him down the road.

"All the museums are free so you can just choose which ones you want to see," Zayne said.

"How much time do we have?"

Zayne raised a brow at him, making him smile bashfully.

"I kinda want to see all of them," Nash said.

"We have all day, babe."

Nash grabbed his hand, dragging a laughing Zayne with him down the street. Everything was new and amazing to him, but Zayne gladly indulged him as they went from museum to museum.

They didn't make it back to the apartment until after nine pm and by then, Nash's legs were protesting from the amount of walking they'd done. Making it up the stairs proved a challenge and once they reached the right floor, he was panting, his hands on his thighs as he leaned forward.

"You okay?" Zayne asked, stopping next to him.

"With the amount of sex we've been having, you should think I'd be in better shape," Nash said, pushing himself upright.

Zayne's laughter brought a smile to his face. Before they reached the door, it was pulled open. Nash blinked at the woman in front of him. She was simply stunning. She was like a female version of Zayne, those exact same eyes and hair color, the same posture. There was no doubt she was Zayne's sister.

"Em," Zayne said and wrapped his arms around her. He lifted her off her feet and swung her around. She made protesting sounds but from the look on her face, she didn't actually mind. When Zayne put her back on her feet, she pushed him out of her way so she could see Nash.

"Hi. I'm Nash," he said, walking closer to shake her hand.

"Emery. It's good to meet you, Nash."

"You, too."

"Well, come on in," Emery said and stepped into the apartment to let them in.

They walked inside and sat down on the couch while Emery went to get them something to drink. When she came back, she gave Nash a beer and when

Zayne reached for the other one, she moved it out of his reach, saying "You're driving."

"Yeah, tomorrow," Zayne whined. He waved her closer. "Gimme a beer, woman."

Emery sighed dramatically at Zayne and handed him the other beer. She walked to a glass cabinet and pulled out a bottle of Jack Daniels and a glass. She sat down next to Nash and poured herself two fingers worth.

"You give us the beer and save the good stuff for yourself?" Zayne asked.

Emery gave him a pointed look and said, "You wanted the beer."

Zayne waved a finger at her accusingly. "You tricked me."

Emery burst into laughter. She turned to Nash, still chuckling. "Works every time."

Zayne mumbled something Nash didn't quite catch but it seemed Emery heard as she flipped Zayne off.

"You can keep your beer," she said to her brother and turned her gaze on Nash. "You, I'm willing to share my 'good stuff' with."

"The beer is fine, thank you," Nash said, a smile on his lips.

"How did you guys meet? My dumbass brother has been extremely tightlipped about you two," Emery said.

Nash threw a questioning glance Zayne's way and when Zayne nodded, he turned back to Emery. "I'm a paramedic and we met when I was out on a call," Nash said, unsure of how much he should tell her.

"He's the one who responded when Grizz fell," Zayne said.

"Wait." Emery held up her hands, her eyes shooting from Nash to Zayne. "Grizz's heart attack brought you guys together?"

Zayne shook his head and said, "I guess, but we kinda met later that day, too."

"In a grocery store's parking lot. I gave him my number." He glanced at Zayne, a smile playing on his lips. "It took him almost a week to call me."

Emery chuckled and said, "Sounds like my brother, all right."

They talked for a bit, Nash enjoying Emery and Zayne's banter. It was nearing midnight when Zayne got a call he had to take. Zayne grabbed his phone and placed a kiss to Nash's cheek before standing and walking out into the hallway.

"I have to ask." Emery lifted her legs up onto the couch and folded them under her as she put her attention on Nash. "How do you feel about his club? Especially with your job?"

Nash shrugged. "I'm not sure yet. I haven't had much to do with the club yet, and he hasn't exactly told me much. I'm not too worried about my job, though. I kinda want to see what happens with us before I do or say anything there."

Emery nodded thoughtfully.

"How do *you* feel about it? The club?" Nash asked.

Emery's face softened. "They're like a second family to me," she said. "I know what they stand for and I know they'll always have my brother's back. And there is absolutely no judgment. Trust me, if I wasn't here, there's no other place I would be than in that club."

Zayne

Nash had already gone to bed when Zayne was done with his phone call, so he went to say goodnight to Emery. She gave him a long hug, telling him how much she'd missed him. Then he walked to the guest bedroom that doubled as an office and closed the door behind him. Nash was in the bed, looking at something on his phone but as soon as Zayne began undressing, Nash forgot all about his phone. Zayne could feel Nash's eyes on him and when he looked up, Nash was watching him closely, his bottom lip between his teeth. Zayne crawled under the blanket and moved closer to Nash.

"Thank you," Nash said, confusing Zayne.

"What for?"

"For taking me here. For letting me meet Emery."

Zayne felt a smile pull at the corner of his mouth. He put his elbow on the bed and rested his chin in his hand.

"Thank you for not thinking I'm crazy for bringing you here," Zayne said.

Nash laughed and pushed at Zayne's chest. Zayne put his hands over Nash's, making the man follow when he rolled onto his back.

"You're not crazy," Nash said, a playful smile spreading on his lips. "A little unhinged at the most."

Zayne reached up to put a hand over Nash's mouth, shushing him. Nash laughed, pulling Zayne's hand away to lean down and kiss him. Nash kept the kiss chaste which was probably for the best. They wouldn't be doing much of anything with his sister in the next room.

"As much as I've enjoyed spending this much time with you, I do need to find a part-time job," Nash said. He wrinkled his forehead. "I got laid off from my last one because I couldn't take the same shifts every week. I was a little busy with my day job, saving people, but he had no understanding of that."

"What an ass," Zayne said.

"You have no idea," Nash said with a heavy sigh.

Zayne rolled them over so Nash was underneath him. "I can always pay you for spending time with me," Zayne said and leaned down to press his lips against Nash's.

Nash hummed against his lips and lifted a hand to slide his fingers into Zayne's hair. "As much as I would like that, I'm pretty sure it's prostitution."

"I won't tell if you don't."

Nash's chuckle made Zayne smile.

"I don't need nor want a sugar daddy. I like making my own money." Nash got quiet for a moment. "I haven't asked before because I've just been enjoying the time we've spent together, but how come you've been able to get that much time off? You do have a job, don't you?"

"It's complicated," Zayne said.

Nash's eyebrows shot up. "How so?"

"I'm the road captain, so some of my time goes to that. The rest is split between our three businesses, whichever one I'm needed at. You know, we might actually need someone at the auto repair shop. Lennox is always complaining about not having enough time to do the administrative work."

"You have an auto repair shop?"

"The club does," Zayne said with a nod. "I can always take you there so you can meet Len and find out exactly what she'd need you to do."

"Sounds good, but uh, who's Len?"

"She's Rooster's old lady."

Nash blinked his wide eyes up at him and he had to laugh when Nash asked, "You have a rooster?"

Zayne shook his head and said, "No. We have a guy whose road name is Rooster."

"How the hell did he end up with a name like that?"

"You don't wanna know," Zayne said.

Nash raised a brow at him and when Zayne didn't say anything, he let out a sigh.

"Well, okay then. Let's go meet Len," Nash said.

A smile tugged at Zayne's lips and he leaned down to kiss Nash. The lips against his were soft and pliant. Nash's fingers slid through his hair as Nash moaned contentedly. Zayne stole another kiss before pulling back. Nash rolled onto his side and Zayne slid closer, pressing his front to Nash's back and placed a kiss to the back of Nash's shoulder.

Nash

He woke to the delicious smell of bacon. He groaned and turned onto his back, reaching for Zayne but all he found was an cold, empty bed. A sigh fell from his lips and he rubbed his eyes before opening them and sitting up. He got out of bed and found a pair of pants and a t-shirt to put on before making his way into the kitchen.

He was surprised to see Zayne at the stove. In the time they'd known each other, he hadn't seen Zayne cook once. Zayne looked over his shoulder, a smile forming on his lips when he saw Nash.

"I figured this might get you up," Zayne said.

Nash walked up behind Zayne, wrapping his arms around him and leaning his chin against the back of Zayne's shoulder.

"You gonna give me some of that?" Nash asked.

"You'd better save some for me, too."

Nash glanced over his shoulder to see Emery walk into the kitchen.

"Hi, Em."

"Morning," she said with a warm smile.

"Don't you have work? What time is it?" He looked at his wrist, forgetting that he wasn't wearing a watch and then looked around to find a clock.

"It's only half past seven. She doesn't have to leave for another hour."

Nash hummed thoughtfully. "Plenty of time to get some good stories outta her."

"Don't you dare," Zayne said.

Emery chuckled and winked at Nash. He helped carry the food to the table and then they all sat down. He poured bacon, toast, and scrambled eggs onto his plate. He dug right in, moaning at the delicious taste.

"You should make me breakfast more often," Nash said to Zayne.

Emery snorted. "He only made the bacon. Or I should say, he put it on the frying pan and for once didn't burn it."

A snort of laughter escaped Nash. "I take it back. Em, *you* should make me breakfast more often."

"Get my brother to come here more often and we've got a deal," Emery said.

Zayne shook his head at Emery, a fond smile on his lips, and when his gaze landed on Nash, he winked. Nash smiled and went back to eating. When they'd all emptied their plates and Nash's stomach was almost too full, he leaned back in his chair with a satisfied sigh.

"What was Zayne like as a kid?" Nash asked Emery.

Emery looked up at Zayne for a moment before returning her gaze to Nash. "Pretty much the same as now. He's always been a bit of a daredevil. A *ride or die* kinda guy. He's also loyal to a fault."

"You make it sound like something bad," Zayne said.

"It's not all bad," Emery said with a shrug.

Emery let out a yelp and glared at Zayne. Nash couldn't help his laughter when he realized Zayne had kicked Emery under the table. The two of them bickered goodheartedly until Zayne's phone rang, dragging him out of the room.

"Have you met his best friend yet?" Emery asked.

Nash turned his gaze on her and shook his head. Zayne hadn't really told him much about any of his friends. He'd told him some about Emery before they planned the trip but other than that, he'd kept most of it to himself.

"Well, when you do meet him, just know that he's always a dick and seriously, don't take it personally if he's all standoffish and rude. That's just how he is with most people. Especially when he doesn't know them," Emery said.

"He sounds like a..." Nash trailed off.

"Complete ass?" Emery suggested. She grinned, shaking her head. "Don't worry. I'm telling you so you hopefully don't dump my brother based on his choice of friends."

Something in the way she said it made him think it had happened before.

"Someone's actually done that?"

Emery nodded, a somber expression on her face.

"Well, first of all, that guy must've been fucking stupid. Who the hell does something like that?" Nash shook his head, getting angry on Zayne's behalf. "Second, Zayne's really gotta mess up good before he gets rid of me."

"I'm glad to hear that," Emery said.

Nash helped Emery carry everything to the sink and just as he was about to help her do the dishes, Zayne reappeared and took the dishtowel from him.

"Go get ready. I left a towel for you in the bathroom," Zayne said.

Nash stole a quick kiss from Zayne and went to their room to grab his bag. Zayne's looked like it was already packed. He walked to the bathroom, stopping in the hallway when he heard Zayne and Emery laugh. He felt a smile widen his lips and shook his head. He found the towel Zayne had left for him on the sink. He stripped out of his clothes and got in the shower. He didn't take long getting showered and dressed and when he was done, he went to their room to grab Zayne's bag. He stepped back into the hallway, both bags in hand and closed the door after himself.

"You ready to go?"

Nash turned, looking up at Zayne who was standing in the doorway to the kitchen, an easy smile on his face.

"Am I ready to hold onto you for two hours?" Nash nodded. "Oh, yeah. I think I'm ready."

Emery pushed past Zayne to get into the hallway. "I like him," Emery said to Zayne and then winked at Nash. "You should keep him."

Emery walked toward him, so he put the bags on the floor and wrapped his arms around her. She squeezed him tightly before stepping back.

"It was lovely to meet you. Please do come back and take my dimwitted brother with you," Emery said with a teasing smile.

"I will. Thank you for letting us stay here," Nash said.

"Anytime."

He waited while Zayne and Emery said their goodbyes and then he handed Zayne his bag. Zayne opened the front door and stepped to the side to let Nash out first.

"Bye, guys. Drive safely," Emery said with a little wave before closing the door.

"Your sister likes me," Nash said with awe in his voice.

Zayne put an arm around Nash's shoulders, pulling him toward the stairs. "Of course she does. What's not to like? You're handsome, smart, brave, and pretty good in bed."

Nash was chuckling as he said, "Yeah, I think I'd be a little worried if she liked that last part."

Chapter Eight

Zayne

HE PULLED up in front of the auto shop. He turned off the engine and waited for Nash to get off the bike before he swung his leg over. He pulled his helmet off and put it in the saddlebag. He took Nash's hand in his and led him inside.

They'd spent the night at Nash's apartment after returning from Washington. Knowing that not only did Nash like his sister, his sister liked Nash as well, made him want the man in his life that much more. Seeing Nash all excited about Washington and experiencing everything with him like it was the first time for himself too, was pretty special.

Walking through the garage door, he glanced around the place in search of Lennox. His eyes landed on the boy who was sitting in a corner on a blanket, looking completely lost in the colorful book he was reading. A smile found his lips as he watched the boy for a moment. Lennox and Rooster had two kids. Jonah was the youngest at five and he loved going with his mom to work. He'd never seen the kid as excited about anything as he was with the cars and bikes coming into the shop. Well, maybe except with his books. He loved those too.

"Hey, Len?"

Lennox's head popped out from behind an open car hood. A smile widened her lips when she saw him and she walked toward them, drying her hands off in a towel she then slung over her shoulder.

"Hey, Saint."

She was a sweet woman with short, blonde hair and a will of steel. She ran the auto shop with a firm hand. Zayne led the way to her and wrapped her up in a hug. Then he stepped back to let Nash introduce himself.

"Hi. I'm Nash Holland."

"Lennox Villa," she said and shook Nash's hand.

"It's nice to meet you."

"You, too. Did Saint tell you anything at all?" Len asked, a knowing smile playing on her lips.

Nash smiled back at her and said, "Not really."

Len tsked at Zayne who just shrugged. She grabbed Nash's arm and tugged him toward the office, saying, "Come on, I'll show you everything."

Zayne knew Nash was in safe hands, so he walked to the kitchen where he found Joker and Hawk. They both turned their attention on him when they heard him enter the room. Hawk frowned at him and asked, "What are you doing here?"

It was a valid question. He knew both Joker and Hawk helped Len out from time to time while he usually worked at the gym or tattoo shop if either place needed an extra set of hands.

"I'm here with Nash. He's talking to Len about doing some administrative work for her," he said.

"You're giving him a job here?" Hawk asked with a raised eyebrow.

Zayne shrugged, saying, "He needs a part-time job and Len needs someone to help out in the office."

"What the hell are you doing, Saint?" Joker growled. "I thought he was just a booty call."

Hawk snorted, making Joker turn his gaze on him.

"He wouldn't have brought a booty call to Talyssa's," Hawk said.

Joker's head snapped back toward Zayne. "You took him to Talyssa?"

Zayne breathed out a sigh. He'd known Joker wouldn't take it well.

"She needed help and he was the only one I could think of with the right qualifications," Zayne argued.

"He's a paramedic. He might as well have been a cop. He's not going to stick around. Not with us and certainly not for you," Joker said.

Zayne flinched. That hurt, and from the ashamed look on Joker's face, he knew it too.

"Look." Joker stepped closer, lifting a hand as if to touch Zayne, but he quickly changed his mind and dropped it again. "I'm sorry. I didn't mean that you don't deserve him. But you know people like him don't want anything to do with people like us. Or if they do, it's only to get their rocks off. To live out some stupid fantasy. They're never here to stay, and I don't want you to get hurt."

"I appreciate you looking out for me, brother, but don't you dare say something like that about Nash again. You hear me?"

Joker nodded, his jaw clenching. "I hear you."

He watched as Joker turned and walked out of the room. Zayne squeezed his eyes shut, rubbing the bridge of his nose as he sighed.

"Beer?" Hawk asked as he rose from his chair to walk to the fridge.

"Yeah. What the hell," Zayne said.

Nash

He followed Len down a small hallway with a door to each side. Len opened the door to the left and waved him inside. It wasn't that big of a room but even with the wide desk, two chairs, and a bookcase, it didn't feel crowded.

"This is where it all happens," Len said.

He turned to her with a smile and said, "It looks great."

"Do you have any experience with administrative work?"

"Yes, I do. I used to help my dad with everything back when he owned a men's clothing store," Nash said.

"When was this?"

"From when I was twelve and up until three years ago when he sold the store. He pretty much taught me everything about running a business."

"If you can answer the phone, book appointments, get the tax stuff sorted, and do my bookkeeping, you're hired," Len said.

Nash's lips twitched, spreading into a smile. "Sounds good to me."

"So which days can you be here?" Len asked.

"It changes every week. Is that gonna work for you?"

Len gave him a wide smile and nodded. "Yeah, sure. As long as I don't have to get near anything tax related, I'm fucking peachy."

Nash breathed a sigh of relief. "Great. I'll just send you my schedule and I guess we'll work it out from there?"

"Sure. That'll be fine," Len said.

Someone called Len's name from the garage.

"I've gotta go see what those assholes have gotten themselves into, but if I know Saint right, he'll be in the kitchen shooting the shit. It's just straight ahead and then the second door to the right," Len said.

"Alright. Thank you, Len."

"You're very welcome." Len shook his hand and they both stepped out of the office. "I look forward to working with you, Nash."

"Me, too."

Nash continued down the hallway and just as he'd passed the first door, someone walked out of the second. It was a man about his height, though his shoulders were wider, and he had short, light brown hair and deep blue eyes. He stopped in front of Nash, his eyes swiping over him from head to toe. Nash opened his mouth to say hello but was cut off.

"You have no business being here."

"Excuse me?" Nash asked, his eyebrows shooting up.

"You have no idea what you're getting into. Do yourself a favor and piss off before you get in too deep."

Before Nash could say anything, the man pushed past him.

"Nice to meet you, too," Nash mumbled.

From Emery's description of Zayne's best friend, he figured this guy could be him. He let out a breath and shook his head. Emery hadn't been wrong about him being an asshole. He just needed to remind himself that it wasn't as much about him as it was about the other man. He walked into the kitchen to find Zayne sitting at a table with the guy who'd been at Talyssa's when she'd given birth. Both of them looked up when they heard him.

"Hey," Nash said.

"Nash. Good to see you again," Nic said as he stood.

Nash smiled and said, "It's good to see you, too. How's Talyssa and Nicoleta?"

"They're both doing well, thank you."

"Good. I'm glad to hear that."

"I guess I'll see you around," Nic said and arched a brow at him.

"Yeah."

Nic nodded, a friendly smile on his lips as he said, "That's good. Take care, Nash."

"You, too."

Nic walked out of the kitchen and Nash turned a glance at Zayne who was staring after Nic, looking baffled.

"I don't think he's ever been so… *friendly* with anyone he doesn't know before," Zayne said.

"What can I say? People like me," Nash said with a shrug. "Except for that one guy before. He does not seem to like me. At all."

"What guy?" Zayne asked, anger lacing his voice.

"The guy I bumped into in the hallway. I'm pretty sure he's your best friend."

"Joker? What did he say?"

Nash turned his gaze to the ground. "He just more or less told me to get the hell away from you," Nash said.

"It's a good thing he's already gone, or I would've kicked his ass for talking to you like that," Zayne raged.

Nash took a step closer to put his hands on Zayne's chest. When Zayne's eyes met his, he said, "It's a good thing he doesn't have a say in our relationship. He doesn't get to tell us how to live our lives."

"You're damned right he doesn't."

Zayne raised a hand to cup the back of Nash's neck. Nash wasn't surprised when Zayne lowered his head to press their lips together. Nash moved his hands from Zayne's chest to wrap around his neck as he leaned into the man. The kiss got rougher as Zayne walked him backwards. Zayne's tongue slid against his, fighting for control. Zayne pushed him against the table, his mouth moving to that spot below Nash's ear.

"I want you," Zayne said against his skin.

"Right now?" Nash rasped. "We're in a kitchen. In your friend's place."

"Does it look like I care?"

Zayne

He unbuttoned Nash's pants, pulling down the zipper. He slid a hand inside, palming Nash's hard length through his boxers. Nash hissed, his fingers digging into Zayne's shoulders.

"What if someone walks in? What if they hear us?"

"They don't care," Zayne said, glancing up to meet Nash's eyes.

Nash looked unsure and he didn't like that. Not one bit.

"You know the word 'no' right?"

Nash nodded before saying, "Yes."

"Good. Just checking," Zayne said and pressed a kiss to Nash's lips.

He pushed Nash's pants and boxers down, his gaze locked with Nash's as he knelt in front of him. Nash's cock was hard and leaking. He gave Nash a wicked smile and leaned down to suck one ball into his mouth. Nash clamped a hand over his mouth to muffle his shout, the other grabbing at Zayne's hair. He played around with Nash's balls for a bit before turning his attention on Nash's cock. He wrapped a hand around the base and licked around the head before sucking it into his mouth. The fingers in his hair tightened, the sting making him harder.

He looked up, meeting Nash's eyes, and took his cock to the back of his throat. The look in Nash's eyes was one of pure lust. Whatever Nash had been concerned about, it looked like it was long forgotten now.

He sucked Nash's cock, loving the sounds Nash made. He put two fingers into his mouth next to Nash's dick, getting them wet, then he moved them between Nash's cheeks.

"Fuck, Zayne," Nash panted, his hips bucking forwards.

He pushed a finger into Nash and let him fuck his mouth. He pumped his finger in and out of Nash's tight hole. His dick was pushing against the zipper of his jeans at the sensual sight that was Nash. He added a finger and Nash thrust harder, fucking himself on Zayne's fingers while Zayne sucked his cock. The head of Nash's dick hit the back of his throat and he swallowed around it, making Nash cry out. He loved how Nash surrendered to his desires, how he seemed to forget everything but the two of them.

His fingers found Nash's prostate and it was clear from the curses falling from Nash's lips that he was getting close. He doubled his efforts, wanting to see Nash in the throes of pleasure. Wanting to make Nash lose control.

Nash tugged on Zayne's hair, making his eyes shoot up to meet Nash's heated gaze. Nash's grip on his hair tightened and his hips bucked. Nash threw his head back, crying out as he came. Zayne swallowed every drop.

He let Nash's cock slip from his lips and was promptly pulled to his feet. Nash's mouth came down on his, Nash's tongue demanding access. Nash sucked Zayne's lip between his teeth and bit down, then soothed the sting with his tongue.

Nash's eyes were dark, almost black, when he put a hand on Zayne's chest to push him a step back. Nash pulled his pants up and then he got on his knees in front of Zayne. The dark and hungry look in Nash's eyes made Zayne's cock strain against his jeans. He needed his pants off and Nash's mouth and hands on him. Nash seemed to be on the same page as he reached for the zipper on Zayne's jeans, pulling it down. Nash got Zayne's pants and underwear down to his thighs and then he wrapped a hand around Zayne's cock. He licked over the head, dipping his tongue into the slit. Then he ran his tongue up Zayne's length.

Nash wrapped his lips around Zayne's cock, taking him to the back of his throat. Nash's fingers gripped the back of Zayne's thighs. He looked up at Zayne but didn't move, his intent clear to Zayne.

"You want me to fuck your mouth?" Zayne asked.

Nash's only answer was to hum, sending vibrations through Zayne's cock and making him hiss. He held onto the back of Nash's head and thrust his hips forward, starting out slowly. His cock slid inside that gorgeous, hot mouth.

"You look so damned good on your knees," Zayne said.

Nash looked up at him with heat in his eyes. Zayne liked that look on him, liked that he was the one putting it there.

Zayne pulled almost all the way out and thrust in deep. Nash gagged on his cock, but he didn't back off, so Zayne kept going. He dropped his gaze to watch his cock slip in and out of that gorgeous mouth.

"Fuck, baby. That's it," Zayne panted.

Nash's nails dug into his thighs, mixing the pleasure with pain and pushing him that much closer to the edge. He pumped his hips, fucking Nash's mouth, the dark look in Nash's eyes spurring him on.

His thrusts grew harder and more uncontrolled as his balls drew up. His orgasm swept over him, Nash's name falling from his lips. Nash kept sucking until his dick became too sensitive and he pulled out of his mouth. He leaned back against the table, his legs a bit unsteady. Nash pulled Zayne's pants back into place, then he stood, and Zayne reached for him, pulling him against his chest. He was still breathing heavily, his arms hanging loosely around Nash's waist. Nash pressed a kiss to the side of Zayne's neck and leaned his head against Zayne's shoulder.

They stayed like that until they'd both caught their breaths, then Nash leaned back in Zayne's arms. Zayne ran his eyes over Nash, licking his swollen lips. Nash looked debauched in the best way possible.

"I can't believe we just did that," Nash said.

"If you wanna be with me, that's gonna happen," Zayne said, searching Nash's eyes for any regret.

"All the time?" Nash asked, his voice rising.

Zayne shook his head. "Not all the time. I won't maul you in the grocery store if that's what you think. But when we're at the clubhouse or here, or anywhere affiliated with the club, I might want to stake my claim. You can say no. I'll always respect your wishes. I promise you that." Zayne cocked his head to the side as he ran his fingertips down Nash's throat. "But I have a feeling you won't be saying no anytime soon."

Nash's Adam's apple bobbed, and he licked his lips almost nervously.

"I don't think I will, either."

Chapter Nine

Nash

STARTING WORK at a place where he'd had sex was somewhat daunting. He walked through the garage door and looked around for a moment to see if anyone else was there. He didn't see anyone, so he figured it was only Len so far. He walked inside just as Len came out of the kitchen, a glass and an apple in hand. When she noticed him, she gave him a warm smile.

"Morning, Len."

"Morning, Nash. You ready to get started?"

"You bet."

Len continued toward a corner of the garage where Nash noticed for the first time that a kid was sitting on a blanket, his nose buried in a book. He'd been there the last time, too. Len crouched down to put the glass down on the floor and handed the boy the apple when he put down his book. Nash walked up to them and Len glanced up over her shoulder at him.

"Nash, this is my son, Jonah. He usually stays here when I'm working," Len said.

"Hi, Jonah."

Jonah looked up at him with wide eyes. Nash recognized the kid's unease, so he crouched down and sat on the floor. Jonah was still looking at him like he might be dangerous.

"My name is Nash," he said in a soft voice. "I saw you reading a book last week. Was it good? I've been looking for something to read and you look like you might know some great books."

Jonah was beginning to relax a bit and when he reached for his book, there was a spark in his eyes. Jonah opened the book and showed Nash the first page.

It was a picture book about a little, blue car and the adventures it went on. Jonah began showing him more pictures in the book. Nash glanced at Len to make sure she was alright with it and the adoring look on her face told him she didn't mind one bit. After a while, he let Jonah get back to his book and stood. Len motioned for him to follow and he walked with her toward the office.

"Thank you," Len said. "He doesn't like strangers and most people act like assholes when he doesn't talk to them. Like it's their fucking right."

"I know the type," Nash said with a shake of his head.

Len led him into the office where she handed him a key.

"That's for the office. I like to keep it locked when I'm not using it. The shop will always be open while you're supposed to be here so no need for a key to that," Len said.

Nash pocketed the key. Len walked behind the desk and sat down in the chair.

"Let me show you how the booking system works," Len said and waved him over.

He stood behind her, looking over her shoulder as she showed him everything on the computer. It looked pretty straightforward. It didn't take long before he felt secure in his abilities to handle it. Len pushed the chair back and stood so he could take the chair. He sat down and rolled it closer to the desk, adjusting the height to fit him. Len walked around the desk, a contemplating look on her face, making him ask, "Is there anything else?"

"This place is owned by the club, so even though everything is legit, shit might go down here," she said.

"Like what?"

Len pursed her lips and shifted her weight from one foot to the other.

"The cops might come here. To search the place and whatever. They'll never find what they're looking for, so no need to worry 'bout that. But someone else might show up and not the friendly kind if you know what I mean." Len walked to the bookcase on Nash's right and grabbed the side, pulling on it. The whole thing swung outward, revealing a small, gray room on the other side. "If you hear an alarm, gunshots, or screaming, you go in here. The backside is made of bulletproof material and it can be locked from the inside."

"That's a bit… excessive."

He wasn't sure what to think about the whole thing. Confusion and concern whirred in his mind. Len pushed the bookcase back into place and said, "We don't exactly live in the best town."

He'd treated enough gunshot victims to know how true that was. But even knowing that, he felt a bit out of sorts. What exactly did Zayne's club do that warranted a bulletproof room in an office?

"I'll let you get to it, then. I don't really have the time for this stuff but I'm meticulous in everything I work with so you shouldn't have any problems, but if you do, I'm just down the hall."

With that, she walked out and closed the door after her. He spent the next few hours learning how everything worked and taking phone calls from frustrated car owners. He was used to dealing with people during some of their worst moments, so this was nothing.

There was a knock on his door and when he looked up, it was to see a young man with dark hair and brown eyes standing in the doorway.

"Len said to come get you for lunch."

"Oh, sure." Nash stood, then paused to shut down the computer. When he stepped out of the office, he shut and locked the door after himself.

Nash shook the man's hand, saying, "I'm Nash."

"Yeah, I know. Everyone knows. Well, everyone here. Len told us you were coming. I'm Jet, by the way."

"Nice to meet you, Jet." Nash cocked his head to the side. "I don't think I've met anyone named Jet before. Is it short for something?"

"Yeah, it's short for Jet Fuel."

Nash blinked at him. "Someone named you Jet Fuel?"

Jet shook his head, a chuckle falling from his lips.

"Nah, man. It's my road name. Everyone at the club calls me Jet."

"Why?"

Jet smirked and said, "I think that's a story for a different day."

Nash was smiling to himself as he followed Jet to the kitchen. Four people were seated at the table. He and Jet sat down in the last vacant chairs. He smiled when he caught Len watching him.

"How's it going? I'm surprised I haven't heard from you yet," Len said.

Nash shrugged and said, "You've made it very easy for me."

There were three men besides himself and Jet. Two of them were twins. One had a piercing in his eyebrow and the other had colorful tattoos peeking up from under the black tank top he was wearing.

The one with the piercing leaned forward and said, "I'm Sully and the less handsome version of me over there is Jack."

"We're identical, dumbass," Jack drawled.

The two began bickering and Nash watched them for a moment before redirecting his attention to the other man. He was a Hispanic man with piercing gray eyes and a neatly trimmed beard.

"Better get used to that. Happens all the time with those two. I'm Walker, by the way," he said and reached across the table to shake Nash's hand.

"So, are you all in the club?" Nash asked, looking around the table.

"I'm the only one who isn't," Walker said and shrugged. "Guess that makes two of us now."

"For now," Jet said only loud enough for Nash to hear.

Nash smiled to himself. Even if these people had saferooms in their place of work, he'd only encountered one of them who was unwelcoming. Everyone else had been kind and helpful. Knowing what they'd done for Talyssa, he couldn't think of them as the big bad criminals Ford had painted them as.

Zayne

He'd been called back to the clubhouse after he'd picked up Nash from the auto shop. He'd only just had time to drop Nash off at home. He'd barely gotten to ask Nash how his first day at the auto shop had been. He'd planned a nice evening for the two of them, but it would have to wait. To say that he was a bit frustrated was an understatement. He tried not to let it show but from the frown Addison was aiming at him, he was being a bit of a grump.

"What's up your ass?" Addison asked, sitting down next to him at the table.

Zayne grumbled under his breath. He groaned when he caught Addison's smug smile.

"Or is the problem what's *not* up your ass?"

"Don't you have something better to do? Like run a tattoo shop?"

Addison huffed. "King called me in. I left Scar in charge."

Zayne's lips twitched at the thought of the small, timid woman trying to control the knuckleheads that were Bones and Juno. They were all amazing artists and tattooists and the times he'd spent at the shop, he'd noticed how well the three of them worked together. The shop was Addison's baby. She did like sharp things after all. He remembered four years ago when she came up with the idea and King supported it wholeheartedly. He'd never seen her as excited about something as she'd been about the tattoo shop.

He heard the door open and looked up to see Joker walk inside, Gabriel right behind him.

"Hey, you guys get called in, too?" Addison asked when they walked up to them.

"Yeah," Gabriel said and pulled out a chair. "But I'm not holding out hope that he called me here for anything but to tell me to go pick up my sister."

A smile teased Zayne's lips as he said, "The curse of being the president's son, huh?"

Gabriel grunted. "Curse sounds about right."

The sound of footsteps from the second floor made them fall silent. King came down the stairs, a grim expression on his face. He walked up to the table and put his hands down on the tabletop. Everyone knew to keep their mouths shut until King had spoken.

"You probably haven't heard yet, but there was a shooting close to Dara's school less than an hour ago," King said.

"What?" Gabriel exclaimed. "Is she okay?"

King nodded and said, "She's fine. A little shaken up, but she's a strong girl."

"Why are we here?" Addison asked.

"You're here because I know who did it and I don't want these fuckers in my town. They need to learn that they can't just do whatever they want here. Actions have consequences," King said.

They all made sounds of agreement. The Kings didn't tolerate outsiders in their territory, and they worked hard to keep the streets clean and safe.

"Gabe. I need you to go home," King said.

For once, Gabriel didn't protest, he just nodded, a grim expression on his face. Gabriel stood and just as he was about to walk away, King laid a hand on his shoulder, pulling him into a hug. They embraced for a long moment before King stepped back to let Gabriel go.

"Stiletto," King said and turned his gaze on her. "Find out where they got their weapons from. I've got a video of the shootout and their guns don't look like anything that gets sold here. I wanna know how they got that shit into Baltimore."

"You think the mob sold the guns to them?" Addison asked.

King shook his head. "No. I already talked to Serrano and he's assured me it wasn't them. He wants to know who they got the guns from, too. He wants them stopped as badly as I do."

If the capo was talking to King and actually agreeing with him, that shit had to be serious. King handed Zayne a piece of paper. On it was scribbled two names and one address.

"Joker. Saint. I need you two to work your magic," King said.

"With pleasure," Joker said, rubbing his hands together with a smile that made him live up to his nickname.

Joker dished out the crazy and Zayne reeled him back in when it was over. It was how it'd always been, from the time they were just reckless teenagers to when they were in the Army. It still was.

"You good?"

Zayne glanced up at Joker and nodded. "Yeah, I'm good."

"Then let's get a move on," Joker said.

Zayne pushed his chair back and stood. He followed Joker to their bikes where he showed him the piece of paper. Joker took it from him and pulled out a lighter. He set the paper on fire and let it burn for a few seconds, then dropped it on the ground. Once there was nothing but embers left, Joker stepped on it.

They shared a brief look before getting on their bikes. Where they were going, they'd need to have each other's back. West Baltimore wasn't a place you wanted to be even during the day. If the guys who'd shot at Dara's school were from the west side, he had no idea what they were doing on their side of town. Either way, those assholes should've known better.

Zayne followed Joker as he pulled into a driveway a block from the address King had given them. They needed to do some reconnaissance before they went in, guns blazing. He hated leaving his bike out on the street, but they didn't have much choice. No residents would touch them, but gang members might if they were crazy enough.

They moved closer but stayed out of sight from the house on the address. Four guys were sitting outside in lawn chairs, one rangy teenager and a boy around ten years old hanging around them.

"Who the hell are they?"

Joker shook his head. "I don't know but they sure as hell have a lot of firepower for some dumbasses shooting at each other outside a school."

"Why the hell would they shoot at each other?"

"Beats me," Joker said with a one-shouldered shrug.

"It doesn't make sense," Zayne said.

The sound of a motorcycle made Zayne tense up. It was coming from the opposite direction than they had, so at least whoever it was wouldn't see his and Joker's bikes. They waited with bated breath as two motorcycles pulled up in front of the house. As soon as the men got off their bikes, their backs turned Zayne and Joker's way, they knew who they were dealing with.

"Whatever they're doing, they're doing it with the Henchmen," Joker said.

"Shit," Zayne mumbled.

The gang members all had their guns drawn as if expecting the worst from the Henchmen. Zayne watched as one of the guys walked toward the two bikers. Zayne squinted, trying to get a better look at the man's face. It took a minute, but he recognized him.

"I know that one. He's a West B. Jackal," Zayne said.

"Well, fuck me if he isn't. I thought they were done."

"Most of them died along with the Destroyers. I guess they've been rebuilding and forming new business relations."

The Jackals were a local gang that did most of their business in drugs and prostitution. It was only half a year ago that they'd been prospecting in a motorcycle club called the Destroyers. No one was really sure what had gone down, but he did know a cop had been killed along with most of the Jackals and Destroyers. The cops hadn't been too kind to any motorcyclists after that.

They waited and watched while the two Henchmen and what looked to be the new leader of the Jackals argued. The Henchmen ended up leaving in a fit of anger. The Jackals headed into the house, while Zayne and Joker prepared to make their move. They circled around the house, not wanting to go in from the front. They'd have better odds moving in from behind.

There was no fence save for the rotten one lying on the ground. They walked onto the deck, their guns drawn. Zayne held up a closed fist, telling Joker to wait. He grabbed the door handle and pushed down gently. The door opened silently, and Zayne threw Joker a grin over his shoulder. Zayne moved, opening the door to let Joker in first, then he followed. He kept his footsteps as quiet as possible. They made their way through the house methodically, until they reached the living room. A TV was on and all four men were there. Just as they were about to enter the room, one of the men stood. Joker waved Zayne back. They retreated just in time for the guy not to see them.

Zayne pressed his back against a wall and waited, listening for the man. When he walked through the doorway, Zayne grabbed him. He pressed his arm against the man's throat, cutting off his air. In ten seconds, the man was unconscious, and Zayne lowered him to the ground. Joker opened the nearest door and after looking inside the room, he waved Zayne over. Trying not to make too much noise, he half carried half dragged the man into what turned out to be a bathroom. He put him down in the middle of the room. Joker walked over and patted the man down. He removed a gun from him and then they stepped out of the room. Zayne took the key from the inside of the room and locked the door from the outside. With the man secured, they moved closer to the others.

"Hey, Tavon? What's taking so long?"

"Tavon is otherwise occupied at the moment," Joker said, stepping into the living room.

"Don't even think about it," Zayne growled, pointing his gun at the two men seated on the couch. All three raised their hands and Joker ordered them to put their guns on the floor one at a time.

"Deon? Jamal?" Joker asked.

Neither moved but it was clear from the look on their faces that it was them. Zayne walked up to the one closest to him and leaned down, putting them face to face.

"So, which one are you?"

"Jamal," he said but not before glancing at the guy who had to be Deon.

That told him Jamal was looking to Deon for guidance, which meant Deon was likely in charge. It only confirmed what he'd seen earlier with the Henchmen. Zayne shared a quick glance with Joker who seemed to have made the same conclusion.

"Back to school day, huh?" Joker tsked, shaking his head at them. "Too bad that school is in our territory."

"Fuck," the third guy mumbled and threw Deon a nasty glare.

"Fuck is right. You messed up," Zayne said.

Deon tried to go for his gun, but Joker didn't hesitate to put a bullet in his thigh. Deon cried out and doubled over. Joker grabbed him by the hair, pulling him upright. Deon's hands went to the armrest, his fingers digging into the fabric. When Joker released him, he didn't move a muscle.

"You're smart enough not to want a war with us, aren't you?" Joker said, pressing the muzzle of his gun into Deon's wound.

Deon jerked, cursing loudly, but he didn't move his hands from the chair.

"This is your one and only warning," Zayne said. "We won't be as polite next time."

Joker put his gun under Deon's chin, forcing his head back. "There won't be a next time, will there?"

"No," Deon said, his voice laced with pain.

"What were you doing with the Henchmen?" Zayne asked.

Deon and Jamal stayed quiet, but the third guy seemed to have a bigger will to live.

"They paid us to guard something. Didn't tell us what."

"Shut your fucking mouth, Marcus," Deon snapped.

Zayne walked closer to Marcus and asked, "Why'd you shoot at each other?"

Marcus threw a glance at Deon, then shook his head. "We didn't. We don't know who they were, we just got the hell outta there."

Well, that wasn't as much help as he'd hoped. The Henchmen weren't exactly stupid. Of course, they didn't share any information with their hired help. Whatever the Jackal's had been guarding, chances were they'd already moved it.

"If you ever see a Henchman in this city, you let us know," Zayne said.

"You expect us to work for you?" Jamal spat.

"No. But if you want to keep this little scrap of town you call yours, you'll have to play by our rules. 'Cause, you see, we are willing to let you do your thing on this side of town but if we ever see you on our side again, we'll be shooting first and there won't be anyone left to answer questions."

There wasn't any need for further words, so they left, taking the men's guns with them. They walked out the front door, Zayne pulling his jacket tight against the wind as the door slammed behind him. All he wanted right then was to go home to Nash, pull him close, and spend the night pressed against him.

Nash

It was late in the evening when there was a knock on his door. He stood from the couch, a frown forming on his forehead. He walked to the front door and when he saw Zayne through the peep-hole, he hurried to open the door.

Zayne's eyes met his, burning with desire. He didn't get a single word out before Zayne's mouth was on his. The kiss was desperate, and Nash welcomed it happily. The door slammed closed. He was too focused on what Zayne's hands and mouth were doing to care. Zayne kissed his way down Nash's neck.

"I didn't think I'd see you tonight," Nash said between gasps. "Not that I'm complaining. At all."

Zayne pulled back, his dark eyes meeting Nash's gaze. "I missed you."

That answer made his heart flutter in his chest. He didn't get to say anything before Zayne's mouth was back on his. Zayne's tongue pushed past his lips, owning him. A hand on his chest made him take a step backward, putting his back against the wall. A wave of desire coursed through his body, his cock hardening in his pants. He forgot how to breathe when Zayne kneeled down in front of him. There was something incredibly erotic about seeing the man on his knees. Zayne reached for the waistband of Nash's sweatpants, his eyes locked with Nash's as he pulled them down, freeing Nash's cock.

Zayne wrapped a hand around Nash's dick, lowering his head to run the flat of his tongue over the veins. Zayne licked up the pearl of pre-come on the tip. Zayne kept his eyes on Nash's as he swallowed him down, taking him to the back of his throat. Nash slid his fingers into Zayne's hair and held on. Zayne's eyes fell shut and he moaned around Nash's cock. Nash's hips jerked, attempting to thrust into Zayne's mouth but Zayne had a hand on his hip, holding him in place.

Zayne pulled back, then sucked him in deep, swallowing around the head of his cock and making him cry out. He watched himself slide in and out of that sexy, talented mouth. His gaze moved down. Zayne had unzipped his pants and taken his cock out, jacking it furiously as he sucked Nash's dick. The sight set his body on fire.

"Fuck," Nash said on a gasp. "I love your mouth. So fucking good."

Zayne moved the hand on Nash's hip to play with Nash's balls, then stroke the sensitive skin behind them. Zayne drew back to suck on the head of Nash's cock, then let it slip from his lips to dip his tongue into the slit. A long moan fell from Nash's lips as he felt his orgasm building fast.

"Zayne. Close," he panted, pulling on Zayne's hair.

Zayne didn't budge, he just kept going. The thought of Zayne taking his load pushed him over the edge. He moaned long and loud as he came, shooting down Zayne's throat. He was unsteady on his feet, glad he was leaning against the wall or his legs would've given out by then.

Zayne pulled Nash's pants back into place. Nash tipped his head to watch Zayne who was getting up off the floor, looking just the right kind of ruffled. His eyes landed on the come covering Zayne's hand.

"I wanted to do that," Nash said.

Zayne's lips quirked at the corners. "You'll get to do it later."

Nash grabbed Zayne's hand, pulling it to his mouth. He licked across the palm, the salty taste of Zayne's come hitting his tongue, then he sucked one of his fingers into his mouth.

A groan fell from Zayne's lips. "You'll definitely get to do that later."

Nash let Zayne's finger slip from his lips and cupped Zayne's face, taking his mouth in a deep kiss. Their tongues tangled languidly for a long time before Nash pulled back.

"I'm looking forward to later."

A smile formed on Zayne's lips and he lowered his head to kiss Nash.

Zayne went to the bathroom while Nash grabbed two bottles of water from the fridge. He put them on the nightstand and took his clothes off. He got under the blanket and had just settled against the headboard when Zayne walked into the room. Zayne took off his cut, folding and placing it on the chair in the corner.

"I thought you weren't going to wear that here?"

Zayne's eyes met his as he turned around.

"I came straight from the club. Didn't really have time to take it off. I wasn't thinking about anything but you."

Nash swallowed hard at the look Zayne was giving him. "You know, you don't have to take it off when you come here."

"Really?" Zayne tilted his head to the side. "You'd be okay with that?"

"You're only taking it off for me, right?"

At Zayne's nod, Nash said, "Yeah, I'm okay with it. It's who you are."

The warmth in Zayne's gaze made him smile shyly and glance down, though only for a second. Zayne pulled his shirt over his head and threw it on the floor. Nash ran his eyes over him. The muscles on that man had drool pooling in his mouth.

Zayne crawled onto the bed, scooting over to sit next to Nash who handed him a bottle. Zayne thanked him and drank down half of it. Nash took a few sips of his own before sliding down in the bed. Zayne looked down at him, an easy smile on his face.

"Why do you shave your head?" Zayne asked, his brow furrowing as he ran a hand over Nash's head.

Nash tilted his head to the side to look up at him and said, "Because I've got crazy curls and not enough time to take care of them."

"Not enough time?"

"Not enough patience. Do you know how long it takes for it to dry?" Nash huffed. "Besides, if I grew out my hair and didn't take care of it, my mom would whup my ass."

"I'd like to see you with curly hair," Zayne said.

Nash shook his head. "I'm sure my mom would love to show you pictures of me as a kid."

"I'm sure she would." Zayne ran his fingers down Nash's jaw. "Will you grow it out for me?"

Nash pursed his lips. "I'll consider it."

Zayne looked satisfied with that answer. He laid down and Nash rolled onto his side so they were face to face. He liked having Zayne in his bed, but he'd never been in Zayne's. He didn't even know where it was.

"Am I ever gonna see your place?"

Zayne's eyebrows shot up. "I live in a two bedroom apartment with Joker," Zayne said.

Nash pulled a face, making Zayne chuckle.

"Yeah, I didn't think you'd want to go there."

Nash sighed, shaking his head. He moved onto his back. Zayne pushed up onto his elbow and leaned over Nash.

"Did you think I didn't want to take you there?"

Nash grinned and said, "I was starting to think you had some other guy stashed away in your apartment."

Zayne snorted. "As if. There's no one but you, baby."

Chapter Ten

Nash

HE GOT up to take a break to rest his eyes from the computer screen. He still hadn't gotten used to staring at it several days a week. He also knew not to stay seated for eight hours at a time. He stretched his back, unsurprised when he heard a few pops. He grabbed his keys and made sure to lock the door to the office before making his way into the garage.

Len had brought Jonah and he was busy getting into trouble with Jack and Sully. Walker was yelling at them, though it didn't seem to have much effect. Nash chuckled at their antics which earned him a middle finger from Walker. He couldn't see Len or Jet anywhere, so he made his way to the backdoor. There was a small alley behind the shop where he knew the others liked to go on their breaks.

He found Jet with a cigarette between his lips while Len was leaning back against the wall, talking to a young man with black hair. Nash ran his eyes over him, and they caught on the vest he was wearing.

"Hey. I thought I might find you two out here," Nash said as he walked up to them.

The man looked up, his dark brown eyes warm when they landed on Nash.

"Hi, I'm Gabe."

"Nash."

Len gave Gabe a clap on the shoulder and said, "Gabe here is a prospect in the club. He's also our president's son."

"It's great to finally meet you," Gabe said.

Nash frowned and glanced at Len. "Has everyone heard about me?"

Len's chuckle made him shake his head with a sigh.

"No. Not everyone," Len said.

Gabe snorted. "Pretty much everyone knows. Auggie's got a big mouth."

Nash raised a brow and said, "Well, that's just wonderful."

"Don't worry 'bout it. Most of us are just glad to see Saint happy for a change," Gabe said.

Nash felt a frown settle on his forehead. "What do you mean?"

He looked between Gabe and Len, settling on Len when she cleared her throat.

"When he first joined the club, he was a bit out of it. He'd just been discharged from the army and he kept almost everyone at bay."

"Him and Joker sometimes just live in their own little bubble," Gabe added.

"Joker," Nash mumbled. "The best friend who hates me."

"Joker hates everyone," Jet said.

"Everyone 'cept for Saint," Gabe added, a wistful smile on his lips.

Nash didn't know what to make of that.

"Joker isn't really good at letting people in, but he's also the kind of guy who, once you've proved yourself to him, will always have your back," Gabe said.

"Yeah, but good luck proving yourself to him," Jet said and got an elbow to the ribs from Len.

"Ouch," Jet yelped, rubbing his side as he stepped away from Len. "What'd you do that for?"

"If you don't know, you should try keeping your mouth shut more often," Len said, glaring at him.

Nash watched Jet as he frowned at Len until he figured out what she meant. Jet made a face and turned to Nash, looking apologetic as he said, "Sorry. I'm sure Joker will come 'round."

"If he doesn't, I know someone who'll kick his ass," Gabe said, a wide smile spreading on his lips. "Saint's sister."

Nash nodded and said, "Yeah. She kinda warned me about Joker."

Gabe's eyebrows hit his hairline. "You've met Em?"

"Yeah. She's pretty cool."

"I know, right?"

It was clear how much Emery meant to Gabe and it was somewhat comforting to him. Even if he never made friends with Joker, he knew he had Zayne's sister's approval.

Len and Jet went back inside but Nash stayed, needing some more time outside to clear his head.

"Hey," Gabe said. "I know you're probably overwhelmed by all this, but you have to promise me you'll give the club a chance."

Nash nodded. "I will."

"Good. 'Cause Saint is worth it."

Zayne

He pulled up in front of the auto shop and no sooner than he'd put the bike on the kickstand, Nash came walking out the door with Len by his side. He took his helmet off, holding it by the strap and got off the bike. Nash was talking to Len and didn't notice Zayne until they were only a few feet apart. He put the helmet on the seat. A wide smile spread across Nash's face as their eyes met. He walked right into Zayne's arms and rested his head against Zayne's chest.

"I've missed you," Nash mumbled.

"You saw me this morning."

Nash pulled back just enough to look up into Zayne's eyes.

"I know."

Zayne moved his hands to cup Nash's face, rubbing his thumbs across his cheeks. Nash grabbed Zayne's vest and pulled himself closer, tilting his head back. Zayne smiled and lowered his head to press their lips together. Nash ran his tongue along the seams of Zayne's lips, and he opened up with a groan. He let Nash control the kiss, happily surrendering to him.

"Bye, guys."

Zayne pulled back and looked over Nash's shoulder to see Len walking away from them while waving.

"Bye, Len."

"See you next week," Nash yelled after her.

Nash turned a sheepish look on Zayne, shaking his head as his lips spread in a grin. Zayne couldn't help himself. He stole another kiss. He leaned back, putting his hands on Nash's hips.

"You wanna go out to eat?"

Nash shook his head. He wrapped his arms around the back of Zayne's neck and leaned against him. "Let's eat in."

"Sounds good to me," Zayne said.

He placed a kiss on Nash's lips before pulling back. Nash called in their order so it would be ready by the time they got there and then they were off. They picked up their food and by the time they walked through Nash's front door, Zayne was pretty eager to get Nash out of his clothes. He kicked the door shut and grabbed Nash by the shirt, pulling him close to put his mouth on Nash's. Nash bit at Zayne's lip, drawing a groan out of him. The take-out bag hit the floor and he pushed Nash against the wall.

They kissed as Nash pulled Zayne's cut off and put it on the dresser. Then Nash's hands were in his hair, making sure he couldn't pull back. Pushing Nash's shirt up, he got his hands on the skin of Nash's back.

What he could only describe as a dramatic throat-clearing pulled them apart. Zayne turned toward the sound and could do nothing but stare. A woman with skin as dark as Nash's and black, curly hair to the shoulders was watching them from the doorway to the kitchen.

"Mom?" Nash exclaimed.

Zayne tore his eyes away from the woman to put them on Nash, blinking slowly at him while he tried to steady his breathing. He shook his head and took a step back to let Nash go.

"Fucking hell, Mom. This is not why I gave you a spare key."

The woman, who was apparently Nash's mother, didn't look the least bit concerned. She eyed Zayne curiously as she walked closer. Fortunately, she hadn't noticed his cut on the dresser, so he moved to stand in front of it. There was no need for her to know her son was dating an outlaw biker just yet.

"Who's this, Nash?"

Zayne stepped forward to shake her hand. "Zayne Lewis, ma'am."

"Oh, please, call me Adisa."

"Mom," Nash said. "What are you doing here?"

Adisa propped her hands on her hips and stared down her son. "You've been ignoring me, so I came here to find out why. Now I know."

Nash turned his gaze on his feet as he mumbled something under his breath. Adisa rolled her eyes and Zayne couldn't stop a smile from spreading on his lips.

"You got enough of that for me, too?" Adisa asked with a nod toward the take-out bag.

"Sure," Zayne said, cutting off Nash's, "No."

Nash glared at him for a second before turning a wide smile on his mother. Zayne was smiling to himself as he watched Nash put a hand on his mother's elbow to lead her into the living room. Zayne carried the food into the kitchen where he grabbed plates and cutlery for the three of them. He was pulling glasses out of the cabinet when Nash walked into the room.

"Why does this keep happening to us?" Nash shook his head, a frustrated sound pushing past his lips.

Zayne turned, leaning a hip against the counter. "I don't remember the last time ending with us having blue balls."

"If this is the universe trying to tell us something, it can shut the hell up and fuck off," Nash mumbled.

Zayne reached out to cup Nash's face. Nash looked up at him with vulnerable, brown eyes.

"I couldn't agree more. But I promise it'll be all right. Granted, this is not how I imagined meeting your mom, but I'm glad to finally meet her."

Nash sucked in a deep breath, letting it out slowly.

"Though, you're definitely gonna have to make this up to me," Zayne said, wagging his eyebrows.

Nash groaned and pushed Zayne away. "Asshole. As if I didn't already have to fight a boner around my mom."

Zayne grinned and grabbed the plates, slapping Nash's ass on his way past. Nash yelped, then cursed at Zayne. Zayne walked into the living room with Nash right behind him. Zayne handed Adisa her plate before sitting down with his own. They ate in silence for a while, but it wasn't long before Adisa's curiosity took over. She put down her fork and turned her sharp gaze on Zayne. "Tell me, Zayne, what is it you do?"

He felt Nash freeze up next to him and he placed a hand on Nash's thigh, squeezing gently to reassure him.

"I do a few different things around town. I teach two times a week in a boxing gym and every other week I do some work in my friend's tattoo shop. But I also do some bodyguarding from time to time. That often takes me out of town though, so I've been taking fewer shifts there lately," he said with a glance at Nash.

It wasn't a complete lie, but he knew better than to tell anyone the truth. Even Nash's mom. He hadn't even told Nash yet. There were too many lives at stake for him to go blabbing to every boyfriend he'd ever had. The difference between those others and Nash was that he actually wanted to tell him. He wanted Nash to be a part of his whole life. Not just the parts away from the club.

"I hear you're a hairdresser," Zayne said to change the conversation.

Adisa lit up in a bright smile. "I am."

"How long have you been doing that?"

"Twenty-four years and I still love it as much as I did when I first started," Adisa said.

"If you're ever in need of a haircut, all you have to do is show up at my parents' place. Mom will take one look at you and pull the scissors out," Nash said.

"I can't help if I love making people look as good as possible. I'd rather give someone a free cut than look at their awful, dry, and broken hair any day. This one refuses to grow his hair out because he thinks it's too much work," Adisa said with a tsk and a shake of her head.

"It is," Nash grumbled.

Having heard that excuse from Nash before, Zayne could only laugh.

Nash

Having Zayne meet his mom was more nerve-wracking than meeting Zayne's sister. Having his mom like who he was with had always meant a lot to him and seeing the way Zayne was with her made him feel all warm and fuzzy inside.

After they finished their dinner, Nash cleaned up while Zayne stayed in the living room, talking to his mom. He didn't feel nervous about leaving them alone. He knew his mom liked to pry but she never pushed when someone didn't want to share something and he had faith that Zayne could handle a prying, overprotective mother.

He was walking back into the living room when his mom said, "So, Zayne. How long has my son kept you from me?"

Nash's snort made Zayne try to hide his laughter with a cough. He walked to the couch and sat down right next to Zayne who wrapped an arm around him. Nash looked up into Zayne's gorgeous, green eyes then turned his gaze on his mother.

"I haven't *kept* him from you, Mom."

"He thinks I'm embarrassing," Adisa said to Zayne.

"'Cause you are," Nash whined.

Adisa waved him off and said to Zayne, "Don't listen to him. I'm awesome and he knows it."

Nash didn't really disagree with her on that, so he didn't say anything. His mom stayed for another half hour in which Zayne continued to surprise him with how sweet and thoughtful he was around her. When they said goodbye, Zayne got a longer hug from his mom than he did. His father was picking her up so she wouldn't have to walk home alone. Nash stayed in the open door with Zayne right behind him while he waited for his mom to make it down the stairs.

As soon as she was with his father, he got a text message from her. He texted her back, put his phone in his jeans pocket and closed the door. He turned, running his gaze up Zayne's body. He licked his lips and reached out to grab Zayne by the shirt. He tugged, making Zayne follow him as he backed toward the bedroom.

"How about we continue what my mom so rudely interrupted?"

Zayne's eyes filled with lust. He reached out to wrap an arm around Nash's waist and stopped him from moving further. Zayne pushed him against the wall, boxing him in with his bigger body. Nash looked up at Zayne, biting his bottom lip.

"I believe you were going to make it up to me," Zayne said with a cocked brow.

Nash felt a playful smile widen his lips. He ran his hands up Zayne's chest to wrap his arms around his neck.

"I could do that or…"

Zayne cocked his head to the side. "Or?"

"*Or,* how about you make me get on my knees for you?"

"I like the way you think."

Chapter Eleven

Nash

ALANNA WAS lying on his bed while he sorted through his closet, looking for the right thing to wear. He figured a pair of jeans was fine, but which shirt to go with it? A dress shirt was way too much, but was a T-shirt not enough?

"So, let me get this straight," Alanna said and rolled onto her stomach, resting her chin on her folded arms. "Your biker boyfriend is taking you to his biker clubhouse to meet his biker friends?"

Nash arched a brow at her. "You're still stuck on him being a biker, huh?"

"It *is* kind of a big deal," Alanna said.

He shook his head and turned back to the shirts, holding up one. He ran his gaze over it and grimaced, throwing it into the pile he was making on the floor.

Alanna sighed dramatically. "Just go with a neutral colored button-down."

"I've got a light gray one," Nash said and searched through his closet to find it. He pulled it out and held it in front of himself to show Alanna. "You think this one would work?"

Alanna gave him two thumbs up, so he put the shirt on the bed and took off the one he was wearing. He put the gray one on and turned to look at himself in the mirror. It was definitely the right choice. He sat down on the bed next to Alanna, a sigh of relief falling from his lips.

"So, your man is into misogyny?"

Nash shook his head. "There are female bikers in the club, and I doubt they'd stand for that. It's not really who they are from what I've gathered."

"Oh, hell. There are female bikers? Don't you dare tell my sister. She'd be all over that. She's totally in a bad girls phase. Driving Dad crazy."

Nash chuckled at the amused expression on her face. Poor Captain Morris had four girls, one worse than the other. Nash raised his hands when Alanna narrowed her eyes at him.

"I won't tell Hazel, I promise," he said with laughter in his voice.

Alanna tsked at him and sat up.

"You promise me to be careful, all right? These guys aren't someone you should mess with and I'd rather get you back in one piece," Alanna said.

"Calm your titties, girl. I'm not looking to mess with anyone."

Alanna flipped him off and said, "Leave my titties out of it."

Nash chuckled and got off the bed. He began to clean up the mess he'd made while Alanna kept him entertained from her spot on his bed. He was laughing at something she'd said about her boyfriend when there was a knock on the front door. He froze, then grabbed his phone to check the time.

"Shit," he blurted. "That's him."

"Already?" Alanna asked, sitting up.

"He's ten minutes late."

Nash hurried to the front door, pulling it open with a wide smile on his face. Zayne looked as sexy as always in his jeans and leather vest. Zayne's eyes met his and then Zayne was stepping through the door, his arms wrapping around Nash. Zayne pulled him close and pressed a kiss to his lips. Nash melted against him. He buried his face in Zayne's chest, Zayne's smell filling his nose as he mumbled, "You're late."

"Only a little. Traffic was a bitch."

Nash leaned back in Zayne's arms and tilted his head up for a kiss. Zayne gladly obliged. The kiss was short but sweet.

"Alanna," Zayne said, making Nash glance over his shoulder to find Alanna standing in the hallway behind them.

Alanna narrowed her eyes at Zayne and said, "Biker." She walked up to Nash and placed a kiss to his cheek. "I'm gonna go, babe. Text me when you get home."

"I will. You do the same," Nash said.

Alanna nodded and went to grab her purse from the bed. She said goodbye, and on her way out, she stopped next to Zayne, glaring up at him.

"If anything happens to my best friend, I'll have the cops on your ass faster than you can say 'not guilty.'"

"Nice seeing you, too," Zayne said to Alanna's back as she walked out the door.

Nash was trying hard not to laugh.

"She's intense," Zayne said.

Nash snorted. "She's a drama queen and fairly overprotective."

"Well, I get the last part," Zayne said and ran his eyes down Nash's body. "You look amazing, by the way."

Nash shifted from one foot to the other, licking his lips. "You look edible."

Zayne's eyes shot up to meet his gaze.

"Nash," Zayne warned. "We have to go."

Nash bit his lip and nodded. He left Zayne by the front door to grab his phone and keys. When he walked back into the hallway, Zayne took his hand, squeezing it gently.

"You ready?"

Nash nodded. "As ready as I'll ever be."

Zayne

Bringing Nash to the clubhouse was a risk, but it was one he was willing to take to show Nash the place he considered home. Nash was on the back of his bike, his arms tight around Zayne's middle and his head rested against his shoulder. He hadn't expected Nash to like riding as much as he did, how much he loved the speed and pressing himself against Zayne.

They drove up to the clubhouse, the gates swinging open for them. He drove inside and parked his bike in its usual place in the row of bikes. He felt Nash get off and pulled off his helmet. He took the one Nash handed him and put them both in the saddlebags. Nash wore a smile that made Zayne's heart flutter. He grabbed Nash's hand.

"Fair warning, babe," Zayne said. "My brothers aren't exactly well-mannered."

"I think I'll be fine. I am used to firefighters, you know?"

Zayne shook his head with a huff. He led Nash to the garage, opening and holding the door for him. Nash walked inside, looking around at the pictures on the wall. There were many, some dating all the way back to when King had first started the club.

"This is where we fix up our own bikes most of the time and both the president and Bandit have offices here," Zayne said.

Nash turned, his eyebrow raised. "Bandit?"

Just then, Auggie popped his head out of his office, a wide smile on his face.

"Thought I heard someone come in," Auggie said. He stepped into the hallway. "I'm Bandit."

Nash ran his eyes over Auggie for a few seconds before shaking his head, a puzzled expression covering his face.

"I thought your name was Auggie?"

Auggie wrinkled his nose at him. "You thought Auggie was my road name?"

"I'm not following," Nash said and looked up at Zayne.

Auggie tsked and said, "My name's August. Auggie for short. But my road name is Bandit."

"Band-Aid," Zayne corrected.

Auggie flipped him off and growled "Asshole" under his breath.

Nash turned curious eyes on Zayne, a brow arched as he asked, "Band-Aid?"

"I'll tell you later," Zayne said.

"All right, then." Nash turned to Auggie. "Um, how's your hand?"

"Much better, thank you."

The clacking of heels against the floor made them all turn. Addison came walking in from the garage, carrying a toolbox. She got a wicked look in her eyes when she noticed Nash.

"Addison," Zayne said with a sigh.

"You must be Saint's paramedic," Addison said to Nash. "He hasn't been able to shut up about you."

Nash's eyes went wide, and he glanced at Zayne who grumbled under his breath and sent Addison a deadly glare.

"Yeah, um, I'm Nash."

Nash had the slightest tint of red on his cheeks as he shook Addison's hand.

"Stiletto, but you can call me Addison."

"Stiletto?" Nash asked.

Zayne grabbed Nash's arm and began pulling him away when Addison opened her mouth to answer. There were some things Nash simply didn't need to know yet.

"Time to go see the clubhouse," Zayne said.

He didn't miss Addison's smirk before he turned Nash and himself around. He led Nash back out the door to the courtyard.

"That was rude," Nash said, pulling his arm out of Zayne's hold.

"Sorry, babe." He wrapped his arms around Nash and pulled him close. "Addison can be a bit intense and I didn't want you to experience that your first time here."

Nash looked thoughtful for a moment before he shook his head, a smile teasing his lips. Zayne lowered his head to press his mouth to Nash's. He felt Nash smile into the kiss as he leaned against him. Zayne cupped Nash's face, running his thumbs over his cheeks.

"Let me show you the rest," Zayne said and took Nash's hand to lead him to the clubhouse.

He opened the door and held it for Nash. They barely made it inside before they were stopped by Jet who ran up to them.

"You're here," Jet said, a big smile on his face. "Finally. I thought he'd never bring you."

Zayne glared at Jet but was only ignored.

"Hi, Jet," Nash said.

Jet wrapped an arm around Nash's shoulders. "Come on, I'll introduce you to the guys."

Nash looked up at Zayne who nodded. Nash went with Jet to the couches where Jet told him everyone's names. From the look on Nash's face, he was trying hard to keep up. Zayne shook his head, smiling to himself as he walked to the bar where Maya was busy pouring drinks and handing out beers.

"Hi, captain. You want something to drink?" Maya asked when he sat down on one of the stools. Before he could answer, Maya's gaze went over his head. "Or someone to save your boyfriend?"

Zayne glanced over his shoulder and couldn't fight the smile breaking free. Nash was sitting next to Jet on the couch, his eyes wide as saucers as Chainsaw showed him one of his many battle scars.

"I mean, unless you *want* them to scare him off," Maya added.

Zayne turned back to her and shook his head. "He'll be fine. Just get me two beers."

Maya raised a brow at him and pulled the beers out of the fridge. She twisted the caps off and handed them to Zayne. He thanked her and grabbed them, sliding off the stool. He walked to Nash's side.

"Here."

Nash glanced up, looking relieved to see him, and took the beer. Zayne sat down next to Nash, laying his arm on the back of the couch. Nash scooted closer, putting them right up against each other. Zayne smiled at Nash and wrapped his arm around Nash's shoulders. They stayed there for nearly an hour, listening to his brothers and sisters talk and joke around. Nash seemed comfortable just sitting next to Zayne. He couldn't have asked for more.

The door opened and a voice he knew well filled the room. Nancy was berating poor Jordan who'd obviously messed up somehow. Nash leaned forward, looking like he was trying to remember where he knew the voice from. It didn't take long for Nancy to notice him.

"Nash," she exclaimed happily.

She forgot all about Jordan and made her way toward them. They both stood, Zayne shoving his hands into his pockets.

"Nancy," Nash said in greeting.

She pulled Nash into a hug. Nash looked surprised but not the least bit uncomfortable as he hugged her back.

"I'm so glad to see you here," Nancy said. She turned narrowed eyes on Zayne. "I didn't think this one would get his head out of his ass and ask you out."

"Hey, now," Zayne protested.

"I didn't think he would either," Nash said and winked at Zayne.

Zayne grunted as Nancy chuckled.

"While you're here, would you mind taking a look at Anders? He's a grumpy ass who doesn't wanna listen to the doctor," Nancy said to Nash.

A smile pulled at Nash's lips and he glanced at Zayne for permission before agreeing. Zayne watched as Nancy took Nash's hand and pulled him to the stairs, talking amicably while Nash chuckled.

Nash

He'd followed Nancy upstairs to a bedroom Nancy told him was their room at the club. She also told him that Zayne, among a few others, had one too. Anders was sitting on the bed, looking at a tablet. He glanced up when he heard them, a loving smile widening his lips as he laid eyes on Nancy. As soon as he noticed Nash, he let out a groan.

"Dammit, woman," Anders grumbled.

"Don't you take that tone with me," Nancy snapped at him. She walked to Anders' side and waved Nash over. "Sweet Nash here has agreed to look at you."

"I don't need looking at."

Nancy sat down on the bed and gave Anders a pleading look. "For my peace of mind?"

Anders grunted loudly before mumbling, "Fine."

Nash was fighting a smile as he caught Nancy's gaze. She threw him a wink. She knew how to work her husband. The thing was, he was sure Anders knew and yet he did as she asked because he loved her. He'd always wanted that. He'd seen it with his parents and they'd always made him want to find someone who knew and loved him like that. He was hoping he'd found it in Zayne.

With a few complaints from Anders, Nash checked his vitals and asked a few questions to ensure Anders had listened to the doctors at the hospital.

"As long as you follow the doctor's orders, you should be alright, Anders," he said.

"Thank you, sweetie," Nancy said before turning to Anders and slapping a hand on his belly. "See, I told you, you asshole."

He got a text from Zayne, letting him know Zayne was in his room. He wrote back that he was done with Anders and would go to Zayne.

"I'm gonna go. Zayne's waiting in his room," Nash said.

"Sure. Thank you, sweetie," Nancy said and wrapped her arms around him.

He squeezed her tight before letting go and stepping back.

"Take care, Anders."

Anders grumbled something under his breath which got him a glare from Nancy.

"Thank you," Anders hurried to say.

"You're welcome."

Nash walked to the door, grabbing the handle, and then paused. "Um." He turned around.

"Out the door to the right, down the hall to the left and then it's the third door on the right," Nancy said.

"Thanks."

He stepped out the door, closing it behind him. He walked down the hall, trying to remember Nancy's directions. He turned left when he got to the end of the hallway. It was a big place with doors on either side of the hall. From what Nancy had told him, most were bedrooms shared between the club members. Zayne's was his alone, though. He still didn't know a lot about bikers and the club, but Len and Jet had been trying to explain things to him. Zayne had told him a few things too, like how important respect was to them. That they had a bunch of rules they called bylaws. He'd also told him that because he was the road captain whenever they went on any kind of road trip which he called a 'run' he was the one who planned it and rode point with the president.

Nash came to a stop, turning to count how many doors he'd walked past. He was by the fourth door to his right. He hesitated but then he heard someone speak from inside the room. If it wasn't Zayne, he could at least ask which room was his. He knocked twice on the door before opening it. He'd only just stepped inside when he froze, his eyes wide. A man was on his knees on the floor, surrounded by three guys who all had their backs to Nash. Blood was pooling around the man's knees and his face was bruised and swollen. Whatever he'd just walked in on, it looked like it'd been going on for a long time.

"What the hell are you doing?"

The men turned and looked at him with dark, cold eyes. He took a step back, realizing the danger he'd just put himself in. The guy closest to him grabbed him by the front of his shirt and pulled back his fist but the hit never came. Nash opened his eyes to see a hand wrapped around the man's fist.

"Touch him and I will kill you," Zayne growled.

The hold on his shirt disappeared and before anyone could stop him, Nash turned and rushed out of the room. He heard Zayne yell orders at the men. He didn't wait for Zayne to catch up with him. He found the staircase and ran down, his sole focus on getting the hell out of there. He heard his name being called but he only quickened his pace as he headed for the door.

He made it out into the courtyard, throwing a fleeting glance over his shoulder before pushing through the gate. He didn't make it far down the street before he heard a bike revving. He drew his shoulders up to his ears, his jaw clenching. He couldn't think. Couldn't associate what was being done to that poor man with the man he'd come to know Zayne as. It didn't add up. This wasn't how things were supposed to be. Did he even know Zayne at all? The thought scared the shit out of him. Who had he let into his life? Near his mother? No, Zayne wouldn't hurt him. Wouldn't hurt his mother. He was sure of that. But everything else? He didn't know what to think, how to feel about it.

"Nash."

He glanced to his left. Zayne was on his bike, driving up next to him. Nash turned his eyes straight ahead.

"Get on the bike, Nash," Zayne growled.

He ignored Zayne and kept walking. He wasn't going to get anywhere near Zayne again. He'd been a fool to think Zayne was any different from the other bikers. He should've known better.

A hand caught his arm and he was shoved against the hard brick wall. His hands were raised above his head, held in a tight grip around his wrists. He struggled furtively against Zayne's hold, his breaths becoming labored and his pulse skyrocketing when Zayne pushed his own body against his to keep him still. He wanted to curse out his body when it instantly reacted to Zayne's proximity. He swallowed hard and tried not to lean into Zayne's touch when he cupped his cheek.

"Don't turn your back on someone as dangerous as me," Zayne said.

"I can't do this. I can't be with you," Nash whispered, surprised at just how much those words hurt to say.

"I know," Zayne said with a defeated sigh. "It's alright. I would never force you into the kind of life I live."

When Zayne let go of him, Nash had to bite his tongue not to beg him to put his hands back. He knew he needed to get away from Zayne because the man was toxic to him. Zayne drew him in, made him feel like no man had before. As much as he didn't want to let that go, with what he'd just seen, he couldn't justify staying with Zayne.

Zayne shrugged out of his cut, then took off his jacket. He laid it around Nash's shoulders and put the cut back on. Nash pulled the jacket tight around himself, trying and failing not to breathe in Zayne's scent on it.

"Let me drive you home?" Zayne asked, pain showing clearly in his eyes.

How could he say no to that?

He nodded and followed Zayne to his bike, taking the helmet Zayne handed him. He put his arms into the sleeves of the jacket, tugged the helmet over his head, and got behind Zayne, wrapping his arms around his waist. He leaned against Zayne, squeezing his eyes shut. He'd never known how riding a bike would make him feel so free, how addictive the rush could be. He doubted he could ever ride another bike without thinking of Zayne, without wanting Zayne's body to press against.

They pulled up in front of his building way too soon. He didn't want the ride to end because he knew then that would just be it. He didn't have much of a choice, though. He pulled his helmet off and took a second to gather himself before he swung his leg over the bike.

He glanced up at his building then back at Zayne who was dismounting. Once Zayne had removed his own helmet and hung it on the handlebars, Nash handed him his own helmet. He didn't know what to say, but looking at Zayne right then was just painful, so he opted for not saying anything. He started toward his building but was halted by Zayne's voice.

"Nash?"

The anguish in Zayne's voice hit him hard. He turned, his eyes locking with Zayne's and before he could change his mind, he walked back to him. He cupped Zayne's face in his hands and brought their lips together in a desperate kiss. Zayne's tongue slid against his, exploring and savoring every second, making Nash acutely aware that this was it; their last kiss. He made a sound in the back of his throat, one of grief and need. Zayne held him closer. They kissed until they were both in need of air. He pulled back, leaning his forehead against Zayne's. He squeezed his eyes shut, holding onto Zayne tightly.

"I'm sorry," he said in a low voice.

He didn't look back as he walked to his building, knowing if he did, he might just change his mind.

Zayne

Watching Nash walk away from him was the single most painful thing he'd ever experienced. That, ironically, was the exact moment he realized he was in love with Nash. His heart was hurting, screaming at him not to let Nash go. But his head knew better. If Nash wanted to leave, he would let him. Maybe he should've fought for him, tried to convince him to give him a second chance, but he couldn't in good conscience drag Nash into the club life against his will. Nash had to want it. He had to want Zayne enough to look past his lifestyle and accept who he really was.

He'd thought if he could just introduce Nash slowly to his world, ease him into it, then maybe Nash would see what a wonderful thing it could be. He hated that he never got that chance. Hated that he had to watch the man he loved walk away.

He clenched his hands into fists, anger rising inside him. He turned on his heels and got on his motorcycle. He drove back to the clubhouse, barely aware of the drive there. He parked his bike and pulled his helmet off, leaving it on the seat of his bike. He stormed inside, finding the men who'd been working on the Henchman by the bar. His eyes landed on Bullet.

"What the fuck were you thinking? You fucking knew there was a civilian here," Zayne yelled as he neared.

"You're the one who let him roam around," Bullet said.

"Hey," Addison yelled. She got into Bullet's face, her hands on her hips. "Saint warned us he was bringing a civilian here. All you had to do was lock the fucking door. Actually, you know damned well you shouldn't have been doing anything while he was here."

Bullet's face got red. Mostly with anger, he was sure. The other two were being smart and staying the hell out of it. Bullet should have done the same, especially after he'd almost hurt Nash.

"You broke the rules. I'll have to take action. Just remember, you brought this on yourself," Addison said.

"Like hell, I did," Bullet snarled. "If Saint hadn't brought a fucking civilian here, it wouldn't have happened. But Saint just *had* to show off his boy toy."

Zayne gritted his teeth as he marched toward Bullet. Joker stepped between them.

"That's enough," Joker said, his voice low but powerful. "Everybody out."

Zayne was seething as he glared at the back of Bullet's head. Addison gave Zayne a sympathetic look before following Bullet. It was a small comfort but at least he knew she'd punish Bullet hard.

"You really like this guy, huh?"

Zayne glared at his best friend.

"You think?" he growled.

"Not to say I told you so, but I did try to warn you that a guy like him wouldn't belong here," Joker said.

"He walked in on a bunch of guys torturing a man, who, for all he knows, is just a regular guy. How the fuck would you have reacted?"

Joker stared at him for a long while, his gaze assessing.

"You didn't explain it to him, did you?"

Zayne shook his head. "No. He'd already made up his mind."

"I'm sorry, brother," Joker said, laying a hand on Zayne's shoulder.

Chapter Twelve

Zayne

IT'D ONLY been a few days, but he was spiraling, and he knew it. He wasn't going to do a damned thing about it, though.

He kept his fists up, circling the guy in front of him as he waited for the attack he knew was coming. Zayne ducked under John's arm when he made his first move and landed a blow to his stomach. He moved away from John and waited for him to straighten up. He saw the determination in his eyes. That was what he needed right then. They went a few rounds, both throwing punches, though Zayne landed more.

Zayne got a hit to the jaw before he managed to get the guy onto the ground. John held his fists in front of his face as Zayne kept hitting him. The sound of flesh hitting flesh, the pain shooting through his hands, he welcomed it. Needed it.

"Alright. I think he's had enough," Addison said and pulled on Zayne's shoulder to get him to let go. He did so reluctantly.

He sat back and glared up at Addison while she helped John up. Two other guys came to help him out of the ring and then Addison was back in front of Zayne, a disapproving look on her face.

"Get up," she ordered.

With a grunt, Zayne pushed up from the ground. He followed Addison, ducking under the rope and jumping down from the platform. He headed toward the locker room but didn't get far before a hand wrapped around his arm and pulled him to a halt. He didn't bother arguing with Addison. He knew it would be to no avail. She pushed him onto the bench, and he sat down with a huff. She grabbed his hands, holding them in front of her as she looked them over.

"Look at these knuckles," Addison said with a shake of her head.

"I'll use brass knuckles next time."

"Don't be an idiot."

He looked up at her with a bored expression. She gave him a stern don't-try-that-shit-with-me glare.

"Next time use the damned gloves. That's what they're for," she said.

He doubted she expected him to say anything to that, so he kept quiet and leaned back against the wall. His breathing began to even out and his hands were starting to smart. He didn't care. He'd much rather feel the physical pain than what he felt otherwise.

Addison shifted next to him and he looked up to see Wildcat headed their way. Addison pulled a face and said, "Good luck," to Zayne before hurrying away. Wildcat stopped right in front of him, her arms crossed over her chest as she glared down at him.

"Why the hell are you beating up my customers?"

Zayne sighed. "He asked for it."

"And how, pray tell, did he do that?"

"With his words, kitten," Zayne said, well knowing she might punch him for it.

Wildcat dropped her head back onto her shoulders and sighed heavily.

"Fine," she said, surprising him.

"You're not gonna rip me a new one?" he asked, almost hoping the answer would be yes.

"No. There's obviously something wrong in your head. I'm not down with beating on morons."

"I forgot what a bitch you can be."

"You'd remember if you actually showed up for work," she quipped.

"I've been a bit busy, in case you've forgotten."

She huffed and put her hands on her hips. "Yeah, you're so busy you don't have time to teach a single class, but you've got plenty of time to beat up my clients."

A groan pushed past his lips.

"Oh, yeah. I know you've been here to fight the past few days," she said.

"I'm not exactly in the right mindset to teach anyone anything, in case you can't tell."

Wildcat pursed her lips and ran her eyes over Zayne.

"We'd better get you in the right mindset, then," she said and turned around. "Hey, Joker? Talk some sense into this asshole, will you?"

Joker raised a brow at her but made his way toward them. Wildcat walked off after giving Zayne an I'm-watching-you look.

"What's up with you?" Joker asked, sitting down next to Zayne.

Zayne glared at him, figuring that would be answer enough.

Joker sighed and said, "Right."

Zayne leaned forward and rested his arms on his knees. He ran his eyes over the gym, taking in the ring in the middle, the punching bags to the left, and the large space with padded floor where Wildcat was rounding up a bunch of teenagers. She was the best instructor they had, but she *had* been taught by the best. The gym was managed by Grizz and Nancy and they'd been running it for over seventeen years. It'd been the very first business the club had opened. Wildcat had shown up at the gym almost fourteen years before with no place to go, no people to look after her, and Grizz and Nancy had taken her in. She was their daughter in all sense but biologically and with her father still recovering from his heart attack, she was running the gym for them.

"How long do you think you can keep this up?"

"As long as I want," Zayne said with a shrug.

"I'm not talking physically. I know you're good there. I'm talking in here," Joker said and tapped Zayne's temple.

"Fuck off."

Joker didn't, of course. He remained right where he was, glaring at Zayne.

"I found someone I could actually see myself with. Someone I wanted in my life. That doesn't happen too often for guys like us. You don't know what that's like even though you've got it right in front of you," Zayne shook his head. "You just choose not to see him."

"Gabriel, you mean?" Joker huffed and crossed his arms over his chest. "He's a kid and not to mention, he's the P's son. He would kill me."

"That's not what's holding you back."

Joker looked up, his eyes meeting Zayne's. He knew his best friend well enough to recognize the longing Joker tried to hide. Even from himself.

"I would wreck him," Joker said with a sigh.

Zayne felt his lips quirk and leaned back in his chair. "I'm not so sure about that. You're protective of him. Hell, you keep protecting him, even without King's say so."

"It's not... I just..."

When Joker sighed deeply, Zayne arched a brow at him.

"You know what I didn't hear you say?" Zayne asked. "Not wanting him. Not liking him. Nothing about him not being your type or some other bullshit like that."

Zayne sat up, making sure to keep eye contact as he spoke.

"Don't make the same mistakes as me. You have to start including him. Treat him like any other prospect. Otherwise, we'll lose him. He'll find something else he wants to do more. Someone else. Is that what you want?"

"You're good," Joker said. He leaned back, his brow raised. "Distracting me with my own shit. But don't think for one second I've forgotten where this conversation started."

Zayne groaned and put his head in his hands.

"Get your head on straight. I don't want to lose you out there. I want to trust you to have my back," Joker said.

Zayne glared at him through his fingers before straightening. "I will *always* have your back. Don't ever fucking question that."

Joker shrugged before saying, "Then stop giving me a reason to."

Nash

Walking up to the auto shop felt strange. He had a knot in his stomach. He wasn't expecting to see Zayne there, but he knew the place and the people would remind him of him all day. The garage was empty save for Len's kid who'd claimed his usual corner where he was playing with his toy cars, too busy to notice Nash as he walked by him. He envied the kid being able to disappear into his own little world.

He was almost at the office when the door opened and Len stepped out. Her brows hit her hairline when she saw him.

"I wasn't expecting to see you again," Len said.

"I made a commitment. I'm not gonna quit on you like that just because Zayne and I didn't work out."

Len looked at him with nothing but kindness. She opened the door into the office and motioned him inside. Neither of them sat down, instead, they stood in front of the desk.

"Is a month long enough to find someone else?" Nash asked.

He needed to find work, too, and he didn't want to leave Len without someone to take over before he left. She was stressed out enough as it was.

Len nodded, a sad expression on her face. "It should be plenty of time. I'd rather keep you, though."

"I like working here, Len, don't get me wrong, but…"

Len waved him off, saying, "I know. I get it. Working with or for your ex isn't exactly fun."

"It's not just that," Nash said.

Len raised a brow at him and crossed her arms over her chest. "What do you mean?"

"What they do? I just can't... I'm a paramedic for Christ's sake. I help people," Nash said.

"Your point?"

Nash studied her for a moment, unsure of how much she knew of what happened at the clubhouse. But then he figured if she didn't already know, then she wouldn't be surprised.

"I walked in on three guys beating up someone. I'm sorry, but that's just not something I can condone."

Len sighed and walked around the desk to sit down in the chair.

"One thing you ought to know about my boys is that while they don't exactly follow most of the laws, they will always treat people fairly. If they were beating that guy, then it was because he deserved it."

"How the hell do you deserve something like that?" Nash asked, hearing the outrage clear in his own voice.

Len watching him for a long moment before she said, "Saint has kept the part of his life that's the club away from you. He's kept you away from the beginning. I don't agree with his choices, but I can understand why he made them."

"What exactly are you trying to say?"

"Let's just say, you're not someone who would normally be a part of a motorcycle club. I assume that's why Saint has kept so much from you. The problem with that is that he's not just kept the bad things from you, but the good ones, too. There's a lot more to this life than you know. Don't you think you've been a bit hasty in making a decision about who we are without having all the information first?"

He didn't know what to say to that. It sounded like something his mom might tell him. After she slapped the back of his head, of course.

"We're a one percenter club and you knew that when you got involved with Saint."

Nash opened his mouth, but no words came out. He snapped his mouth shut and turned his gaze on the floor, his shoulders sagging.

Len stood, walking around the desk to put a hand on his shoulder.

"I'll leave you to it, then."

As he watched her walk out the door, he wondered whether she meant the work or contemplating his decision.

Zayne

He sat by the bar, tapping his fingers against his beer bottle. He'd barely slept for days, thoughts of both Nash and the Henchmen keeping him awake. They all knew the Henchmen were up to something. They were moving in on King territory. It was one thing for them to steal from the Kings, but it was a whole other to arm a gang, which, according to Addison's research, was exactly what they'd done. The weapons were a specific kind only the Henchmen sold in the states surrounding Maryland. That, combined with them showing up at the Jackal's place shortly after the shootout at the school, made it clear that they were up to something and his gut was telling him it was something big. He didn't like it one bit. King had even ordered them not to go anywhere alone the next few days, just to be safe.

He threw back the last of his beer and pushed away from the bar, turning to glance around the room. A few of his brothers were sitting on the couch, their old ladies keeping them company. Joker and Addison were at the tattoo shop and he didn't know where Auggie was hiding. But he did know where one person was. He walked outside and headed to his bike. Gabriel was busy cleaning the windshield of one of the cars.

"Gabriel. With me," he ordered.

Gabriel's head shot up, his eyes wide with excitement. He dropped the rag, asking, "Where are we going?"

Zayne ignored him and put on his helmet. Gabriel hurried to get on his own bike. Gabriel was an exceptional rider. He was one of those guys where it just came naturally. He'd seen the kid race and if he wanted to, he could probably make a career out of it. He drove off with Gabriel right behind him.

He pulled up to the building across from Nash's. He parked the bike and walked to the door, glancing over his shoulder to see if Gabriel was keeping up.

Gabriel jogged toward him, a confused expression on his face. Zayne made his way up the stairs to the third floor where there was an unoccupied apartment. He'd picked the lock the first time he'd been there and left the door unlocked each time he'd left since.

He walked through the apartment, wrinkling his nose at the putrid smell there. Gabriel was a bit more vocal about it, gasping and cursing. Zayne ignored him. He pushed the only chair there toward Gabriel. Gabriel didn't sit down, he just grabbed the backrest, his gaze out the window. Nash's apartment was across from them, only a floor lower, but they could still see into his apartment. Nash was in the living room, sitting on the couch with something in his lap. He had no idea he was being watched.

"You know, this kinda feels like stalking," Gabriel said.

"Does your cut say prospect?" Zayne asked without taking his eyes off Nash.

"Uh, yeah?"

"Then shut it."

Gabriel looked at him like he'd lost his mind. He didn't give a shit about what Gabriel thought. He needed to make sure Nash was alright. Especially now with a possible war between them and the Henchmen. He'd ordered Gabriel to go to Len's earlier and to stay long enough to offer Nash a ride home. He wasn't keen on Nash riding with anyone else, but he trusted Gabriel would take care of him.

Watching Nash didn't make the pain go away, but it did soothe his aching heart. At least for a short moment before the pain came back worse than before.

"If you want him back so badly, why don't you fight for him?" Gabriel asked.

"I can't force him into my lifestyle," Zayne said with a grunt.

"But from what I heard, you just let him walk away. You didn't even try."

Zayne's phone beeped with an incoming text and he used it as an excuse to not answer Gabriel. The text was from King, letting him know there'd be church in twenty minutes. He needed to be there, but Gabriel didn't. Leaving him alone did pose a risk but as long as he stayed out of sight until Zayne could make it back, he'd be fine. He didn't think any of them, prospect or otherwise, were actually in danger from the Henchmen. They wouldn't come after them when they were alone. It wasn't their style. Ronin liked to make big statements. Usually with a lot of firepower involved.

"I have to go. Stay on him. I want him watched until this damned threat is over."

"*Yessir*," Gabriel quipped.

He shook his head at Gabriel and with a last, longing glance at Nash's apartment, he left. He took the stairs two at a time and when he reached his bike, he got on and took off.

Chapter Thirteen

Zayne

HE WALKED into the clubhouse and headed straight for the room they always used for church. When he walked in, only half the members were present, so he sat down in his chair and leaned back. Bones and Scar were sitting across from him, talking amicably about something tattoo related. He ignored them in favor of turning to Jet who was busy texting someone.

"Hey, Jet?"

Jet didn't look up from his phone as he said, "I know what you wanna ask and I'm not gonna answer."

"Don't be a dick. I just wanna know how he's doing," Zayne said.

Jet sighed and put his phone in his pocket. He looked up at Zayne, something akin to pity showing in his eyes.

"How do you think?"

"Dammit, Jet. Just answer the fucking question," Zayne snapped.

"You should've talked to him before taking him here. He doesn't know shit about the club life, that's for certain. He was curious before, wanted to learn, but now? I don't think he knows what to say to us. He's not scared of me or the others at the shop, but he seems distant like he's pulling away from us. I'd also wager he's got one hell of a broken heart."

Zayne knew he was glaring at Jet when the guy shrugged and said, "You wanted to know."

He *had* wanted to know but hearing that Nash might be afraid just didn't sit right with him. He had to talk to him. Clear things up. Nash didn't have anything to fear from the club. Or him. He needed Nash to know that he would never hurt him. He'd rather cut off his own arm than lay a finger on Nash.

He was stewing in silence as people started to arrive. Addison sat down next to him and when she tried to talk to him, he ignored her. He needed to think. To come up with a plan on how to make things right with Nash. Maybe even get him back.

"Alright. Settle down," King said, getting everyone's attention. "Our resident Henchman finally started talking and it turns out he had a lot to say."

"Who got him to talk?" Joker asked.

Zayne knew both Hawk and Reaper had tried. So had he. They hadn't gotten much out of the man.

A smile widened King's lips. "Turns out, violence wasn't the way to get him talking. Auggie dug up a few things that made him sing a different tune."

"They've been moving a big supply of drugs into Baltimore and their goal is to distribute to all of Maryland," Auggie said.

Curses filled the room. If there was one thing everyone at the club despised, it was drugs. Especially the deadly shit the Henchmen dealt in.

"They're moving in on our territory? Who the hell do they think they are?" Jack snarled.

"If a fucking turf war is what they want, we'll give 'em one," Joker said, slamming his fist down on the table.

"I think we should start with getting those drugs the hell outta town," King said and stood. "Everyone for doing that, say aye."

There wasn't anyone against, so they went right into discussing how to do it.

"I checked the location he gave me, and it looks like they haven't moved the drugs yet," Auggie said.

"Get me a map," Zayne said to no one in particular.

Jet grabbed a city-wide map from the pile they kept in the corner of the room and rolled it out on the tabletop.

"Where is it?" Zayne asked Auggie.

Auggie scanned the map before placing his index finger on it. Zayne grabbed a marker and drew a circle around the spot. He took a minute to study the location.

"They've boxed themselves in," Zayne said and pointed at the surrounding houses. "They've only got one clear way out, but we can cut them off."

King nodded. "Let's do it."

"All right, everyone who needs to return to work, you can go," Joker said.

It wasn't an all-out war that required everyone there and they did have businesses to run. Len had Walker with her, and King sent Jet back to the shop, too. A few of the others returned to work as well. Hawk and Viper were out on runs they couldn't return from in time to help. The rest of them got ready to ride and once they were, they took off with Zayne in the front.

The first thing he noticed as they neared the address was how close it was to Dara's school. There was no way that was a coincidence. Whatever had happened between the Jackals and the Henchmen was bad enough it'd ended in a shootout. As it was, they were lucky no one had gotten hurt or killed.

He pulled into a parking lot less than half a klick from the address. King who'd been driving right behind him stopped next to him. They got off their bikes and waited for the others.

"Stiletto, Rooster, Chain, you guys secure the area. Call if you see any cops or Henchmen headed this way," King said.

Stiletto gave him a short nod and turned, walking back to her bike with the two others right on her heels.

"Saint, you're on recon," King said.

"Gash, Reaper, with me," Zayne said and walked to his bike, grabbing the binoculars he always had in his saddlebags. They walked the rest of the way so their bikes wouldn't give them away. He stopped two houses over, behind some big bushes, and handed the binoculars to Gash. Zayne checked for parked cars on the properties closest to the house. He'd already sent Reaper to check out the houses with backyards directly against the Henchmen's. They needed to make sure there weren't any civilians near or in the house before they went in.

"I've got eyes on Ares," Gash said.

Ares was the VP of the Henchmen. Zayne had met him on two occasions, and he'd gotten the same impression after each; Ares was a dangerous man. Smart and cautious but also vicious when he needed to be.

"He doesn't look happy."

Zayne took the binoculars Gash handed him. Looking through them, he saw Ares standing on the front porch, looking like he was arguing with the two men in front of him. He watched until Ares and the others disappeared into the house, then he put down the binoculars.

"Do you think there's more than them?" Gash asked Zayne.

"I doubt it."

"Only two guys to watch the house? That's a bit of a risky choice, don't you think?"

Zayne shook his head and said, "This is the kind of neighborhood where people would notice if a bunch of guys were coming and going at all hours. They're trying to remain undetected."

Gash snorted. "They pretty much do. If Hawk hadn't caught one of them, we wouldn't have known about this before their product hit the streets."

"Why hasn't it, though?" Zayne asked. "It has to have been here for a while. One of their guys is missing. Why haven't they moved it yet?"

"You think they're waiting for something?" Gash asked.

"That, or something's been holding them back," Zayne said and pulled his phone out to text Reaper. "Let's see if we can find out."

They made sure to check every possible exit for the Henchmen, though he was more concerned with getting the drugs than catching any Henchmen. They met up with Reaper and then they made their way back to the others where they relayed what they'd observed. They all agreed that now was the time to strike. There was no way of knowing if more men would show up later.

King was looking at Joker as he said, "Try not to kill them. They might have information we can use."

"Ares probably knows a lot more than the two others," Joker said with hope in his voice.

"No, you can't just kill the others. In fact, don't kill anyone," King said.

Joker didn't look happy about it, but he'd do as he was told

"Don't use your guns. If you have to, let them go," King said. "They chose this neighborhood for a reason. These people are more likely to call the cops. Take your cuts off. I don't want any of us connected to this place or the drugs."

"You got it, Prez," Zayne said.

He shrugged out of his cut and put it in one of his saddlebags. Sully was staying behind with the bikes, ready to call in backup or warn them of cops or Henchmen. Zayne followed Joker, the two of them splitting up from the group. They were going in from the back. They had to cross through another backyard to get into the one at the Henchmen's house. There was no car out front and most of the houses seemed empty. It was in the middle of the day, so most people were fortunately at work. They walked to the wooden gate which, they found, wasn't locked. The fence into the Henchmen's property was eight feet tall but at least there weren't any barbed wire or spikes on top. Zayne kept an eye on the house as Joker crawled across the fence. As soon as Joker let him know it was clear, he turned and reached up, grabbing one of the posts. He made his way up the fence and once on the other side, he jumped down onto the ground.

The tiny backyard was empty save for a swing set. They walked up to the patio door, getting on each side of it and pulling out their guns. They didn't have to wait long before they heard shouting and wood splintering. On Joker's signal, Zayne pulled the door open and Joker stepped inside. Zayne followed close behind. He recognized King's booming voice as it echoed through the house.

They were only halfway through the room when someone came running through the doorway. Ares came to an abrupt halt and with a curse, he turned on his heels and ran in the opposite direction. Joker ran after him while Zayne watched his back. They cut Ares off in a bedroom. His only way out was a window or through them.

"Ares," Joker yelled, aiming his gun at Ares' back.

Ares raised his hands and turned around. Zayne laid a hand on Joker's shoulder in an attempt to ground him before he lost control and shot Ares. King didn't want a bloodbath and none of them wanted to fire a gun in this neighborhood. He caught Ares eyeing them curiously before he took a step backward.

"Don't move," Joker barked.

Ares cocked his head to the side, the shadow of a smile playing on his lips. "You're not going to shoot me, are you?"

Before either of them could answer, Ares turned and ran toward the window. He jumped right through it, the glass shattering all over the place. Joker cursed and moved to the window only to stop when Zayne put a hand on his gun and pushed it down.

"Let him go," Zayne said.

They weren't there for him or the other Henchmen. Not this time.

The sound of a motorcycle starting came from just outside the house. Zayne let go of Joker's gun and turned to search the rest of the house. Joker remained right behind him as they went from room to room. They found the huge pile of drugs in one of the bedrooms. Once they'd secured the house, they made their way outside to find the others.

King and Reaper were standing in the tiny front yard, their heads close as they spoke. Gash and Jack came walking in from the road. Zayne followed Joker down the front steps to stand with King and Reaper.

"Ares and the other guys got away," Gash said as he jogged up to them.

"Doesn't matter. We've got the drugs," Zayne said.

"How much?" Reaper asked.

Joker grunted and said, "Enough for all of us to retire right now."

"Let's make sure this doesn't end up in the wrong hands," Zayne said.

"I don't want anyone near this shit," King said.

"We can always call the cops," Joker suggested.

Zayne and King turned incredulous eyes his way.

"And what? Just call them and say, 'Hey, we found this big pile of drugs, do you guys want to come pick it up?'"

Joker shrugged and said, "Maybe we just call in an anonymous tip."

"Fine," King said. "That gets it out of our hands and keeps it out of theirs."

That got him some nods and sounds of agreements.

"I've got the number to the vice department. Give me a burner phone and I'll make the call," Joker said.

Zayne waited for Joker to make the call while the others took off. They were going to wait close by until the cops showed up to make sure the Henchmen didn't get a chance to take the drugs back.

Nash

A throat clearing startled him and almost made him drop the glass of soda in his hand. He put the glass down on the coffee table and glared at Harper who was just sitting down across from him in the armchair.

"What?"

"You're miserable," Harper said.

"Thank you for pointing out the obvious. I so needed the reminder."

"She's right."

He let out a sigh before turning his head to look up at his mom who was walking toward them with the lemon pie Harper and Mel had brought. He bit back the words on the tip of his tongue and stood to help her. He took the pie and the knife from her, setting them on the coffee table while his aunt put down plates for them.

"If you're so miserable without your man, you shouldn't have ended it," Aunt Aliyah said.

"It's not that I don't want to be with him," Nash said with a frustrated breath. "I just can't."

"That sounds like you chickened out," Harper said.

Nash shook his head. He hadn't told any of them the real reason for the breakup. He didn't know how.

"Come on now, Harper. Nash is far from being a coward. You know that," Mom said. She looked at Nash with scrutinizing eyes, tilting her head to the side. "So, tell me, what did this handsome, sweet, and polite man do to make you break up with him?"

"It doesn't matter," Nash mumbled, glancing down at the hands he was wringing.

His mother huffed and said, "Oh, baby, it matters all right. Did he cheat on you?"

Nash's head shot up. "Mom! No. God, no."

"Hmm. Well then, what was it?"

"You're too nosy for your own good," he mumbled.

She snorted. "Baby, I'm a hairdresser. It's my job to be nosy."

"No, it's your job to cut hair."

She hummed and gave him her don't-try-that-shit-with-me look before saying, "And I noticed you started to grow out yours."

Nash let out a groan. He knew there was no way out of that one.

"He wanted me to," he mumbled.

"Damn. I think I like him better now than before," Mom said.

"Momma," Nash whined.

"What? I'm just sayin'."

"Leave my hair out of it," he said, crossing his arms.

"Whatever you say, baby."

Mel was pressing her lips together to keep from laughing so Nash flipped her off, saying, "You're a shitty partner. You're supposed to have my back, not be laughing at me."

"How did I let you talk me into coming here again?" he asked Harper.

Harper raised a perfectly shaped brow at him. "You were walking around like a zombie. All I had to say was 'food' and you were following me."

He crossed his arms over his chest and leaned back in the couch, knowing she was probably telling the truth. He *had* been a bit of a zombie, just going through the motions lately. Not having Zayne in his life anymore had turned out to be much harder than he'd expected. Knowing that Zayne wasn't going to walk through his door in the evening was making him feel restless. He didn't know what to do with himself most of the time.

Nash stayed for another hour, mostly listening to the women talk but he was starting to get tired. He'd had a nightshift at the firehouse the day before and a full workday at the auto shop that day. He said his goodbyes and let himself out of the house. He lived in walking distance from his parents and he knew he could use the air and exercise. It did, however, give him time alone with his thoughts. Of course, they centered around Zayne.

What Len had said to him earlier was very much at the forefront of his mind. Did he owe Zayne a chance to explain? Did he want to give him that chance? Was it too much of a risk to his heart? Maybe he had overreacted. Maybe he hadn't. There wasn't really any way of knowing that without letting Zayne explain the situation.

He drew his shoulders up and shoved his hands into his pockets. He knew the second he spotted the van slowly following him that he was gonna be in trouble. He pulled out his phone, trying to make sure the people in the van couldn't see. His finger hovered over the buttons, unable to move. He knew he should call 911 but his instincts were telling him to call Zayne.

He didn't get to press a single number before arms wrapped around him from behind. He fought back, kicking out and yelling, but they were too strong. He was lifted into the van and pushed into the corner. His phone fell onto a blanket lying next to him, but it didn't seem like any of the men noticed. One was too busy yelling at the driver to get the hell out of there and the other was closing the door. When he turned around, he aimed his gun at Nash's head and said, "Stay there."

Nash's heart was beating frantically in his chest and for a long moment he thought that that was it, he was going to die, but then reality set in. If they were going to just kill him, they would've done it on the street. They wouldn't have dragged him into a van unless they were planning on taking him somewhere. But why would anyone kidnap him? His parents weren't anywhere near rich enough to warrant a ransom, and he was just a paramedic.

He fought to calm down his heart, to slow his pulse and kickstart his brain. He used the breathing exercises he knew. He glanced around the van, taking in everything. Why hadn't they covered his eyes? Why hadn't they covered their own faces? Common sense told him there were only two reasons for that. One, they didn't expect him to report the kidnapping once they let him go, or two, they weren't planning on letting him go at all.

He was still stuck on the why of it all. Why him? What did he have that would make anyone think him of value? He swallowed against the bile rising in his throat. Maybe it wasn't about a what but a who. Only one person came to mind; Zayne.

Zayne

He was waiting with Joker not too far from the house. They had a clear view of the street and the front of the house.

"They're taking their sweet time, aren't they?" Zayne asked.

"I told him it was time sensitive. All we can do is wait and hope the Henchmen doesn't come back with twenty guys to try and take back the drugs."

"Nah, I think they split. They're probably expecting us to take the drugs for ourselves."

Joker nodded and Zayne sighed, leaning a shoulder against the wall. They spent a few minutes in silence, just staring at the house until an unmarked, black car and a patrol car pulled up. They watched as two men in suits got out of the black car and one uniformed officer followed them. They'd left the front door wide open for them and the cops went inside with their guns raised.

"Guess we can go now," Joker said and raised a brow at Zayne. "Unless you wanna wait for them to search the area for criminals?"

"Fuck off," Zayne said and pushed away from the wall.

They drove back to the clubhouse where the others were waiting for them. They parked their bikes and walked inside. They found King, Hawk, Rooster, Auggie, and Addison by the bar.

"The cops have the drugs," Zayne said.

"Good. Great job, guys," King said, slapping Zayne on the back.

Zayne sat down on one of the barstools. "So, are we going to talk about how these assholes got into Maryland in the first place?"

"We need to find a way to make sure they don't come back," Addison said.

"Let's come up with a plan, then," King said.

They began bouncing ideas off of each other. They spent half an hour on it, and they weren't any closer to finding a solution. Not knowing the Henchmen's endgame was making it hard to determine a plan of action. Zayne leaned forward, resting his elbows on the bar top. He got distracted by his phone ringing and after excusing himself, he walked outside to answer it.

"Saint," Gabriel panted in his ear. "They've got him. The Henchmen have Nash. I saw them take him and I couldn't do a damned thing about it. I'm so sorry."

He wasn't sure he was even listening to Gabriel after those four words. He let his arm fall to his side, Gabriel's voice over the phone sounding far away. Breathing got harder as Gabriel's words hit him. They had Nash.

He barked at Gabriel to get back to the club and then he hung up, already running through the door.

"The Henchmen have Nash," he said, still not believing the words even as he said them out loud.

Silence fell over the room. It lasted all of ten seconds before Rooster cursed.

"Auggie, see if you can trace his phone," Joker said.

"You don't think they'll take him to their clubhouse?" Rooster asked.

Joker shook his head. "Too risky and seeing as they took him alive, I'd wager they want to trade him. If they're smart, they aren't going to keep him where we can easily find him. Besides, they know we can get onto their property."

"It's gotta be somewhere close," Hawk said.

"If they tossed his phone, I won't be able to find them," Auggie said.

Every pair of eyes in the room turned to King. Whichever way the club got involved, it was King's decision.

"I hate the idea of making any kind of deal with them, but if we can't find Nash, I'll agree to make the trade," King said.

Zayne knew King would only be doing it for him and it was probably because he knew Zayne would go after Nash on his own if he had to.

"One small problem, guys. We don't have anything to trade with," Hawk said.

"But they don't know that," Addison said.

"They might," Hawk said. "If it was me, I would've circled back to the house. If they did that, they would've seen the cops."

All in all, their odds were shit. Zayne didn't care. All he could think about was getting Nash back. He wasn't going to let anything happen to him. He'd burn down the whole damned city to find him.

"Auggie," Zayne said, a plea in his voice. "Find him."

Chapter Fourteen

Nash

THE ROOM they'd left him in was only lit by the light filtering through the cracks in the door. He wasn't sure how long they'd been driving but he didn't think they'd left town. His hands were bound in front of him and his back was to a wall. The only things in the room were a table, a few chairs, and a cabinet. He knew there were shards of glass somewhere on the floor because he'd stepped on them when they'd walked him inside. He pulled at the rope around his wrists, but it was tied too tight and he knew all he would do was hurt himself if he kept trying. He searched for the glass only to find the pieces too small to cut the rope with.

A frustrated sigh pushed through his lips. How the hell had he ended up in this situation? He didn't have a clue as to what was happening or who these people were except that they were probably in a motorcycle club. He'd noticed the bikes when they'd dragged him inside from the van.

The door burst open and he shrunk back, pushing himself further into the corner. The lamp in the ceiling turned on, blinding him for a second before his eyes adjusted. Two men came into the room, a third man between them. They lifted him up on the table in the middle of the room and helped him get out of his vest and bloodstained shirt.

One man put something resembling a first-aid kit on the table while the other left for a moment only to return with a bottle of booze. If he was planning on doing what Nash thought, he had to do something. No matter what you saw in movies, pouring alcohol in open wounds was a bad idea.

"I can help," Nash said.

They barely spared him a glance. Nash pushed up off the ground and cleared his throat.

"I'm a paramedic. I can help him. Or you can just keep doing what you're doing and he'll probably die," Nash said.

The two men glanced at each other but didn't say anything. The man on the table groaned and pushed himself into a seated position. He had light brown hair and blood trickled down the side of his head. He glanced at Nash, his dark blue eyes moving over Nash's face.

"Let him."

One of the men protested but the guy on the table cut him off, saying, "Get outta here. I'll be fine. Just give me my gun."

Nash waited until the man had the gun and the two others left the room before he walked up to the table. The guy eyed him warily before grabbing Nash's hands to untie the rope. Nash held his breath until he was free. He breathed in deeply before reaching for the medical supplies on the table.

"Lie back down," Nash said.

For a second, Nash thought he wouldn't do as he said but then the man sighed and laid down. Nash stared at the gun in the man's hand for a long second before tearing his eyes away. He knew this could go wrong but he had to at least try. He forced himself to forget about the gun and the situation he was in and went into work mode. He grabbed a pair of gloves and put them on.

"I'm Nash. What's your name?"

"Ares."

Nash ran his eyes over Ares' torso which was covered in small gashes on the right side. Some had glass embedded in them.

"Can you tell me what happened, Ares?"

"Why?"

Nash glanced up from Ares' chest to meet his eyes.

"Why do I need to know what happened?" Nash asked with a frown.

Ares shook his head. "Why are you helping me?"

"I might not be a doctor, but I took an oath, too."

"Do no harm, huh?"

"You know it," Nash said with a nod.

Neither said another word while Nash began picking pieces of glass out of the cuts. He considered asking how it'd happened again, but then thought better of it. Ares didn't make a sound as he dug the pliers into his wounds. Once he was sure all the glass was out, he began cleaning the cuts and assessing which ones needed stitches. Fortunately for Ares, it was only two of them. He searched through the first-aid kit, surprised to find needle and thread. He glanced up at Ares.

"I don't have anything to numb the skin, so this'll hurt. You up for it?"

Ares nodded and said, "Go ahead, doc."

He didn't do too much stitching in general, but his hands were steady, and he knew what to do. It probably wouldn't be pretty, but he had a feeling Ares wouldn't care. When he was done, he took a second to look at the wound at Ares' hairline. It wasn't deep and once he'd cleaned off the blood that had run down Ares' face and into his hair, it looked like the bleeding had already stopped.

"So, doc, am I gonna make it?" Ares asked.

"Yeah. You'll be just fine, provided you've got your tetanus shot."

Ares arched a brow at him and said, "But you told the others I might die."

Nash chuckled. "They had no idea what they were doing and, trust me, they were doing more harm than good."

"Well, then I'm glad we kidnapped you," Ares said with a smirk.

"Please, don't remind me."

He put the supplies back into the kit and pulled out bandages. He put them over Ares' wounds and taped them on. Once he was done, he pulled off his gloves and threw them on the floor.

"There. You're good to go," Nash said and stepped back to let Ares sit up and swing his legs over the side of the table.

With Ares sitting up right in front of him, Nash noticed his muscular chest and arms for the first time. He had a few tattoos down one arm and one across his chest. He also had one on his ribcage which he figured must've hurt like hell. But the man in front of him seemed indifferent to pain.

"Grab that bag on the floor for me?"

Nash's eyes shot up to meet Ares for a second before he turned, looking for the bag. He found it halfway under the table. He pulled it out and lifted it up into Ares' lap. When Ares struggled to open the zipper with the gun in one hand, Nash took over for him but much to his surprise, Ares put the gun on the table behind himself. Nash couldn't help his eyes from shifting to the gun.

"I wouldn't blame you," Ares said.

Nash cleared his throat and stepped back. The last thing he wanted was to get shot because he wasn't careful. He didn't doubt Ares was more than capable of taking a life.

Ares pulled a shirt out of the bag and Nash watched as he put it on. Ares moved the bag from his lap to the table next to him. Nash glanced up, finding Ares' eyes on him.

"What they did? Kidnapping you? It's wrong. It's all wrong," Ares said.

Nash crossed his arms over his chest and glared at Ares. "If it's so wrong, then why did you do it?"

Ares shook his head and said, "I didn't."

That wasn't anywhere near the answer he'd expected. He stared at Ares for a while, trying to figure out if the man was telling the truth. Something inside him told him he could trust Ares, why, he didn't know.

"Do you know why they took me?"

Ares looked at him with a raised brow. "You don't know?"

"Well, I have an idea, but I still don't know why they would take *me*," Nash said.

"You're seeing one of the Kings. Their road captain," Ares said.

"I was. But that ended some time ago."

Ares groaned loudly and for a second, Nash thought he was in pain, but then Ares said, "Those idiots. They kidnapped an ex. No offense, Nash, but your man has probably already moved on."

Nash couldn't help his flinch.

"He means something to you, huh?"

Nash knew he shouldn't be telling Ares anything. For all he knew, the wound was self-inflicted so Ares could get him talking. He figured these guys were crazy enough to do something that fucked up. But Ares put him at ease and, somehow, he felt safe with him.

"Yeah. He means a lot, actually," Nash said.

"He break your heart or something?"

Nash shook his head, a lump forming in his throat.

"More like I broke both our hearts. I thought I couldn't handle his lifestyle," Nash said and laughed until it turned into a sob. "I can't believe I have to go through this and not even have Zayne after. I mean, if we'd still been together…" He shook his head. "I don't even know what I'm saying."

"I think what you're trying to say is that you think all of this would've been worth it if you still had Zayne."

"Maybe," Nash said, glancing down at his hands.

"I'm gonna help you get outta here," Ares said.

Nash's head shot up. "Why?"

"Because you don't deserve being pulled into this shit and I'm fucking tired of doing what Ronin tells me to. He's lost his fucking mind."

Nash frowned, not recognizing the name.

"Come on," Ares said and slid off the table, wobbling for a moment.

Nash grabbed him by the elbow, hissing, "Careful."

"Here," Ares said, pushing something into Nash's hands.

He looked down at what turned out to be Ares' cut.

"What am I supposed to do with this?"

"Put it on."

He jerked his head up, his eyes narrowing on Ares.

"No one will notice you if you wear it. Just don't let anyone see the front," Ares said.

"What about you?"

Ares shrugged. "I'm the VP. They all know what I look like. Even without my cut they won't question me."

Ares slung his arm over Nash's shoulders and Nash put his hand on Ares' hip to support him. They walked out the door and down what turned out to be a long, narrow hallway. He could hear faint voices coming from different directions.

"Keep your head down."

Nash ducked his head and pressed closer to Ares. To anyone looking, it'd look like he was helping Ares walk when really, Ares was the one holding him up. As they moved through the building, he became more convinced it was abandoned just by the state of everything inside. They walked into a more open room where he saw a table, a half-rotten kitchen, and a few chairs scattered around. One of them was occupied.

"Hey, Ares?"

Nash froze. Panic was starting to set in when Ares turned them half around, so Nash was furthest away from the guy who'd spoken.

"What's up, Crank?"

"The P says to be ready. He's set up a deal to trade the fag for the drugs."

Ares cursed under his breath. "Sure. I just need to take a piss then I'll meet you outside."

Apparently, that was all Crank needed to hear because he grunted a non-answer and took off toward a door in the other end of the room. Nash was still somewhat paralyzed when Ares began to move again. Nash was barely breathing as they made their way through the building. Ares was leaning more and more on him.

"There," Ares said, pain lacing his words.

Nash looked up, his eyes landing on a door just down the hall. They just needed to make it out that door. He didn't even know what was on the other side, except a chance to escape. Once they were out, they'd still need a way to get out of there. He tried not to think about their odds. He did know that he wouldn't have stood a chance on his own. He wanted Zayne to come and save him more than anything, but he knew he needed to be realistic about it.

If they made it out of there, he was going to find Zayne. There was a lot they needed to talk about but ultimately, he knew what he wanted. Life was too short not to be with the man he loved.

Zayne

It didn't take Auggie long to trace Nash's phone and from the looks of it, the Henchmen still had it. King called in their brothers and sisters and as soon as everyone were armed, they took off. The whole drive there, he had to remind himself not to drive as fast as he really wanted because he wouldn't be any help to Nash if he was dead.

There were quite a few abandoned buildings and constructions sites in this part of town. Zayne led them to one of the buildings where he knew they could hide the bikes and have a view of the house Nash was presumably in. Everyone made their way to the top floor, stepping over holes in the floor and missing steps.

The room he walked into was filthy and when he pulled down the curtain of a window, dust flew everywhere, making him and a few others cough. He stepped back when Auggie walked up to the window, a tablet in his hands.

"His phone is in that van," Auggie said and pointed toward a black van parked in front of the red brick house.

Zayne was cut off from saying anything by his phone ringing. He didn't recognize the number, so he answered it.

"Who the fuck is this?"

"Saint. We have your boyfriend. If you want him back, do as I say. If not, I'll be sure to mail him back to you, piece by piece," Ronin said. "Check your phone."

Zayne's phone beeped with an incoming text. He pulled the phone away, gritting his teeth when he saw the picture of Nash huddled in a corner of the van. He put the phone back to his ear.

"What do you want?" Zayne hissed.

"I want what's mine. Give it back and I'll let your boyfriend go."

"You want to make a trade?"

"I'll send you the address. Thirty minutes. Come alone."

Ronin hung up before Zayne could say anything. He took a moment to push down his anger before putting his phone away. They'd taken Nash because he was the easiest to get to and they wanted to use Zayne's love for him to make him betray his club. Ronin thought King wouldn't let Zayne trade the drugs for a civilian. Nash was just a boyfriend. One who wasn't really a part of the club. Ronin knew that. It was why he'd called Zayne directly, believing he'd steal the drugs from his club. The worst part was, he couldn't say he wouldn't have done exactly that if things had been different.

"He wants to meet and trade Nash for the drugs. We have to move in now," Zayne said.

"Addison, Zayne, you two take the rear entrance. Reaper, I want you to stay up here, keep that rifle at the ready. Sully, Jack, get to that van. Joker, Rooster, and I will take the front," King said.

Zayne gave King a nod and turned, walking ahead of Addison down the stairs. She stayed right behind him as they made their way around the house to the back. They were almost past the last house before the one Nash was in when he heard a door open. He motioned for Addison to stay back while he peeked around the wall. He saw two men step out of the house, one half behind the other. He recognized Ares, the Henchmen's VP and stepped forward, pointing his gun at his chest. That was, until Nash stepped out from behind Ares and between them.

"Don't shoot," Nash said.

For a long second, Zayne couldn't do anything but stare at Nash. He faintly heard Addison call King to tell him they had eyes on Nash.

"Nash. Move," Zayne barked.

"No. Not until you put your guns down."

"I'll put my gun down if he does," Zayne said.

Nash bit his lower lip, looking conflicted as his eyes darted from Zayne to Addison. Nash turned around, putting his back to Zayne. He was glad Nash trusted him enough to turn his back on him when he was holding a gun, but he didn't like the way Ares was looking at Nash. Not one bit. The fact that Nash was wearing Ares' cut just pissed him off more.

"I won't let anything happen to you, remember?" Nash said.

"Nash," Ares said, his voice hoarse.

"Please."

Ares reluctantly holstered his gun and held his hands up. Zayne lowered his gun. Addison walked up to Nash and Ares, taking Ares' gun and patting him down. When she was done, Ares let his arms fall down and Addison motioned for him to walk ahead of her. Ares raised a brow at her but started walking toward Zayne. As Ares passed by him, his lips pulled into a knowing smile. Zayne clenched his hands, fighting to keep from hurting Ares. Addison looked like she wouldn't mind putting a bullet or two in him herself.

Zayne turned his eyes back on Nash who was walking closer, stopping two feet from him.

"Hey," Nash said, his voice soft. "I wouldn't have gotten out of there without him."

"I know. That's why he's still breathing," Zayne said through his teeth.

He reached for Nash to get him to move but Nash took a step away from him, a hurt look flashing across his face.

"I'm not going with you unless you promise you won't hurt him," Nash said.

"Baby, can we not do this right now? We're kinda in enemy territory," Zayne said.

Nash crossed his arms over his chest and didn't say a word.

Zayne groaned and shook his head. "Fine. No one will hurt Ares. I promise."

The relieved look on Nash's face made him think Nash hadn't been sure he would actually agree to it. He wouldn't have done it for anyone else but Nash.

Nash took Zayne's hand and their eyes met for a few heartbeats. What he saw reflected in those deep brown eyes made his heart beat faster. Nash wasn't looking at him with fear or blame, only warmth.

Chapter Fifteen

Zayne

NASH WAS sitting on his bed, a blanket over his legs. He didn't look too bad even if he was still a bit shaken up. As soon as they'd made it to the clubhouse, he'd dragged Nash upstairs to his room where he'd checked him over for injuries. There hadn't been any except for a bit of redness around Nash's wrists. The thought of Nash having been tied up made him see red.

He was pacing the room, trying to calm himself down. He wanted to go right back there and make those bastards pay. No one hurt the people he loved. No one certainly got away with it alive. Nash cleared his throat, making Zayne stop and look at him. He walked to Nash's side.

"I'm so sorry," Zayne said.

"It wasn't your fault."

Zayne shook his head and sat down on the edge of the bed. "But it is my fault. They wouldn't have gone after you if it weren't for me. Hell, they must've been watching me. Watching us." He clenched his hands into fists. "I should've seen it."

"You can't control what other people do. They would've just taken someone else."

"But they didn't," Zayne said.

"At least it wasn't Len and Jonah."

As much as it hurt to even think about someone hurting Len and Jonah, it was nothing compared to how he'd felt and still felt about the Henchmen taking Nash. It'd been the worst few hours of his life. Not knowing if Nash was alright, if he was even alive. The not knowing was the worst because it made him imagine all the horrible things they could've been doing to Nash. But he'd gotten him back. Nash was safe and that was all that mattered.

"You should get some rest." Zayne stood. "I'll leave."

He walked toward the door.

"I was wrong," Nash said, making him come to an abrupt halt.

He turned around, finding Nash standing, his lip between his teeth.

"I was wrong to leave."

Zayne took a step toward Nash, then stopped, reminding himself what Nash had just been through. He wanted to believe him, but he wasn't sure he could.

"I want you, Zayne. In my bed, but more importantly, in my life," Nash said.

"Now you know what being a part of my life really means," Zayne said, fully expecting Nash to take back his words.

Nash smiled, cocking his head to the side as he said, "I think I handled it pretty well."

He couldn't exactly argue with that, so he didn't. But he didn't move either.

"What?" Nash asked.

Zayne shook his head but said, "I'm afraid you're gonna say yes now and then, later on, you're gonna regret it."

"I will never regret being with you," Nash said and when Zayne opened his mouth to argue, Nash cut him off. "I'm not saying I'm a hundred percent sure that we'll still be together in ten or twenty years. I can't know that, and neither can you. But what I am certain of, is that I'm in love with you."

"What?" Zayne breathed.

"I love you and if you want me, I'm yours," Nash said.

Zayne crossed the room in a second, taking Nash into his arms and crushing his mouth over Nash's. Nash wrapped his arms around Zayne and leaned into him. Zayne licked along the seams of Nash's lips and Nash opened to him with a throaty groan. The kiss started out desperate but got more steady as they explored each other's mouths.

He made quick work of Nash's clothes and then he started on his own, but Nash stopped him. Nash grabbed his vest, pulling it slowly down his arms. Nash's eyes were on Zayne's as he folded his cut and put it on the dresser behind Zayne. Nash moved back in front of Zayne, lifting his hands to run them under Zayne's shirt. Zayne raised his arms to let Nash pull his shirt off. He threw it on the floor and grabbed for Zayne's belt. Zayne put his hands over Nash's, stopping him.

"Get on the bed," Zayne growled.

Nash's eyes darkened with lust and he hurried to crawl onto the bed. He turned, lying down on his back in the middle of the bed. He looked gorgeous like that. Spread out with his cock hard and leaking.

Zayne pulled a packet of lube out of his pants pocket and threw it onto the bed. He unbuckled his belt and pulled it free. He opened his pants and pushed them down, stepping out of them and his socks before getting on the bed. He grabbed the packet and tore it open. He got his hand slick and wrapped it around Nash's cock, pumping his hand a few times before moving it to his own. As Nash looked up at him with heady eyes, he was sure he could come just from watching Nash. The man was gorgeous, and all his.

He leaned over Nash, getting between his spread legs. Nash reached for Zayne, sliding a hand up his neck to the back of his head. Zayne took Nash's mouth in a rough kiss and thrust against him. His dick slid against Nash's, making them both moan. Zayne reached between them, taking both their lengths in hand. He jerked them both, twisting his hand over the heads of their cocks, and earning himself a throaty groan from Nash.

Nash squirmed under him.

"Want you inside me," Nash said, sounding breathless.

Zayne pulled back, reaching for the lube. He poured the last over his fingers and slid them between Nash's cheeks. He circled Nash's hole, teasing until Nash swore at him. With one hand on Nash's thigh, he pressed a finger inside him. He didn't touch Nash's cock and took his time to get him ready, only adding another finger when Nash begged.

Nash pushed back on his fingers. Zayne glanced up at him. Sweat glistened on Nash's skin, his back arched as he tried to fuck himself on Zayne's fingers. His own cock was painfully hard, and he needed inside Nash. Needed to take him, to claim him.

"You ready, baby?"

"Fuck, yeah," Nash said, tilting his head to catch Zayne's eyes.

Zayne removed his fingers and reached for his pants, shaking them to find his wallet. It fell onto the floor and he swiped it up, pulling a condom out of it. He turned back to Nash who'd taken his own cock in hand, his eyes on Zayne.

He got back onto the bed and rolled the condom down his length. He grabbed a pillow to put under Nash's hips, then he lined himself up with Nash's hole and kept his eyes on Nash's face as he pushed inside. Nash bit his lip, his hands fisting the sheet. Nash was panting when Zayne bottomed out. Zayne put a hand next to Nash's head, running the other up Nash's thigh. Nash wrapped his legs around Zayne's waist, tilting his hips and taking him in deeper.

"I'm not letting you go again," Zayne said.

Nash's Adam's apple bobbed as he swallowed, nothing but want in his eyes. Zayne pulled back slowly then thrust into Nash hard.

"Fuck," Nash gasped, his fingers grabbing at Zayne.

He fucked Nash with all the passion, all the anger and frustration he'd felt when they'd been apart. He moved his lips down Nash's jaw to his throat. He kissed and licked his way up Nash's neck.

"You're mine," he growled against Nash's skin.

Nash whimpered. His legs tightened around Zayne's hips, pulling him closer.

"Zayne," Nash begged.

Nash's hands were on him, sliding across slick skin, nails digging in as he held on. Zayne pumped his hips, fiery desire burning through him. He pulled

Nash's hands off him and put them above Nash's head. He laced their fingers together, his thrusts slowing and his kisses turning softer. He leaned back so he could see Nash's face.

"Say it."

Nash's eyes flew open.

"I love you," Nash said without hesitation.

"You're mine, baby. All mine."

"Yours," Nash agreed.

Nash threw his head back, his eyes closed, and his lips parted on a silent gasp. Nash came between them, spurting all over both their chests. Zayne pumped into Nash, chasing his own orgasm. Nash dug his nails into Zayne's ass, the bite of pain sending him over the edge. He thrust into Nash a few more times as he came, then he stilled, putting his weight on Nash while he fought for breath.

Nash was carding his fingers through Zayne's hair while they both caught their breaths. Zayne moved back and kissed Nash, their tongues tangling languidly. Zayne pulled out and discarded the condom. He cleaned them both off and then fell back into bed. He was on his back with Nash lying on his side next to him, running his fingers in circles on Zayne's chest.

"How did you get your road name?" Nash asked, then frowned. "That's what it's called, right?"

Zayne chuckled and reached up to run his fingers along Nash's jaw. "Yeah. That's what it's called."

With everything that'd happened, he figured Nash deserved some answers.

"We're not your average one-percenter club," Zayne began and held a hand up to stop Nash from talking. "Don't worry. I'll get to how I got my name."

Nash laid back, nodding his head.

"A lot of MC's sell drugs or guns. Some are even involved in human trafficking. We have our legal business to keep us afloat, but we have been selling guns at one point. Then, a few years ago we were approached by a man. He wanted our help in transporting something else."

Zayne ran his fingers through what little hair Nash had. Knowing Nash had been growing it out for him, even when they'd been apart, only served to convince him that them being together was right.

"I'm afraid to ask," Nash said.

"Humans."

Nash jerked upright, looking down at Zayne with disbelief and horror covering his face.

"Not the way you're thinking," Zayne said and sat up. "These are people who want our help, who needs it."

"Like Talyssa?"

Zayne nodded and said, "Exactly like her. Except these people come from all over the country. Some even from other parts of the world. This club has always been about helping people. It started out with just helping the members. Most are veterans or people who've had a rough life. People the system couldn't or wouldn't help. Then we began helping others.

"One of the first times I helped someone, it was this old lady from Italy, and she kept calling me Saint but, in the beginning, I just assumed she was mispronouncing my name. Then as I was about to leave, she grabbed my hand and said I was a saint sent to her from God. I was still a prospect then, so King was helping me, and he heard her. He began calling me Saint after that and soon that's just who I was."

"That sounds about right," Nash said, a loving smile on his lips.

Zayne nodded, a sigh escaping him. "That was five years ago."

"Really? When did you become the road captain?"

"Two years ago. I'd been riding a lot with the former road captain and I loved helping him. I've always liked planning things and organizing the club's runs was fun."

"What happened to him?"

Zayne felt a smile tease his lips. "He retired. Just out of the blue. One day at church, he told everyone he wanted me to take over from him and once that happened, he moved to Florida with his wife."

"Do you still keep in touch?"

"Yeah, him and the wife come to visit from time to time. They're both pretty amazing people," Zayne said.

"They sound like it," Nash said.

Zayne nodded and placed a kiss to Nash's lips, then pulled him down to lie with his back pressed against Zayne's chest. He wrapped an arm around Nash, his hand over Nash's heart. Nash laced his fingers with Zayne's. He pressed a kiss to the back of Nash's shoulder and closed his eyes, a smile on his lips as he fell asleep.

Nash

Zayne had brought him breakfast when he'd woken, and they ate together in bed. When they were done, Zayne took everything back downstairs, leaving Nash alone. Nash stood from the bed and pulled on his clothes from yesterday. Last night, he'd heard one of the guys tell two others to put Ares in a room upstairs, so at least he knew what floor to look on. He needed to see Ares, to talk to him and make sure he was alright. After all, the man was there because of him.

He opened the door and stuck his head out. The hallway was empty, so he stepped out and closed the door. He wasn't sure how he'd find Ares but once he turned a corner, he found a man standing in front of a door, his arms crossed, his hip holster and gun visible.

Nash walked up to him and he didn't even have to convince the guy to let him see Ares, he just opened the door for him. He stepped into the room, surprised at how it looked. It was basically like any other room at the clubhouse with a queen-sized bed, a dresser, and a door that led to a bathroom. The only difference was that this room didn't have a window and there was a guard at the door which was kept locked. Ares was lying on the bed, a book in his hands. He looked pretty relaxed for a guy who was being held hostage.

"Hey," Nash said.

Ares looked up over the book, his eyes widening when he saw Nash. He put the book down on the bed and sat up.

"I didn't think your caveman would let you see me," Ares said.

Nash sat down on the bed. "He's not really a caveman. He just doesn't trust you."

Ares watched him with narrowed eyes.

"He doesn't know you're here, does he?"

Nash shook his head and sighed, saying, "No."

"What are you doing here, Nash?"

"I just wanted to make sure he kept his promise, and, I don't know…" Nash shrugged. "Help you get out of here?"

Ares stared at him for a long time. So long Nash got nervous and began fiddling with the bedsheet. Ares laid a hand over his to stop him and when he looked up, it was to find Ares' eyes filled with warmth.

"You're not gonna help me do anything," Ares said.

"But—"

"No, Nash." Ares squeezed his hand, the harsh tone of his voice leaving no room for arguments. "You're a civilian whether Saint likes you or not. You're a paramedic. Don't risk your life for mine."

"You think they would hurt me?" Nash asked.

"Oh, I know they will."

Nash shook his head. "Zayne would never let them. But what am I supposed to do then? I can't just leave you here. What about your club? I got the impression you wanted out?"

"I do, but I don't." Ares shrugged. "It's complicated."

"If there's anything I can do, please tell me. I don't want—"

The door burst open, cutting Nash off. They both turned their heads to a furious looking Zayne.

"Get the hell away from him," Zayne growled, and Nash wasn't sure which of them he was talking to.

Nash stood and took a step away from the bed. Zayne's angry gaze clashed with his.

"What the hell do you think you're doing?"

This time, he knew Zayne was talking to him. He put his hands on his hips and gave Zayne a glare.

"Making sure he's alright," Nash said.

"I promised you no one would hurt him," Zayne said through his teeth.

"I know and I don't think I've thanked you for that, so thank you. But, Zayne, this is wrong. You have to let him go."

"No."

"Yes, you do. Otherwise, you're no different than them," Nash said.

"Don't even try to spin that shit with me, Nash. We're nothing like them and I don't need you saying it to believe it."

"You've made me an accomplice to kidnapping and whatever else you have planned for him. It'll be on me, too. I don't want that on my conscience." He felt like an asshole with what he was about to say, but he knew he needed to say it, even if it wasn't true. "Either he goes, or I do, and I'll go to the police."

Zayne didn't say a word, he just stared at Nash.

"Nash," Ares said, making him glance over his shoulder at him. "It's cute that you want to save me, but honestly, I don't deserve it. Don't ruin what you two have over me."

Nash stared at Ares. The last thing he wanted was to drive a wedge between himself and Zayne, but he also knew he couldn't go against his principles. Not when there were lives on the line. Ares' life.

"He's the reason I made it out of there alive," Nash said in a last effort to make Zayne understand. "I owe him my life."

He saw doubt on Zayne's face. He bit his lip and shook his head.

"I don't want to be making ultimatums and I certainly don't want to risk what we have. But I can't let you do anything to a man who saved my life."

"There's only one way this can go the way you want," Zayne said after a long moment of silence. "Right now, *you* owe him your life."

The way Ares perked up made Nash believe whatever Zayne was about to say was something big.

"I can only let him go if *I* owe him," Zayne said.

"But you don't," Nash said, turning his gaze on the floor.

Hands cupped his cheeks, tilting his head up to meet Zayne's eyes.

"But I could," Zayne said.

"How?"

"You know how Len is Rooster's old lady?"

Nash nodded and put his hands over Zayne's.

"She's also his wife, but here, in the club? Her being his old lady means so much more. No one hurts a brother's old lady and if someone from outside the club risks their lives to save an old lady, the whole club owes them."

It sounded like a perfect solution. On the surface, at least.

"There's only one problem with that. I'm not really a lady," Nash said.

Zayne threw his head back and laughed, shocking the hell out of both Nash and Ares.

"Old man, then," Zayne said with a lopsided smile.

"Who are you calling old?"

"Is that a yes?"

Nash didn't even have to think about it.

"Yes."

The smile spreading on Zayne's face made Nash's heart skip a beat and he forgot how to breathe when Zayne brought their lips together. He slid his fingers into Zayne's hair. He was smiling into the kiss when Zayne pulled back, his eyes on Nash's lips for a second before he glanced up into Nash's eyes.

A sound from Ares made Nash take a step back. Ares was watching them with intense eyes.

"I've heard a thing or two about you guys being pretty inclusive, I just didn't really believe it before now," Ares said.

Nash raised a brow at him and said, "You've known we were together since before the two of us met."

"Yeah, but that's one thing. Saint having you as his old man that's a whole other thing. I didn't think it actually existed," Ares said. "Wouldn't have ended up with the Henchmen if I had."

"Wait. Are you saying you're gay?"

Ares shook his head and said, "Bi. That's how I've made it work in my club."

"That's gotta suck," Nash said.

"Sometimes, yeah," Ares said. He shrugged. "I knew how most people see it in this environment when I joined the club. I was content to keep that part of me to myself. I didn't really care. The club has always made me happy. But lately, everything the club stands for has changed. Ronin has changed everything to suit his needs. He's been branching out, crossing state lines and territories. Then he went as far as to kidnap a civilian."

"You wouldn't have saved me if I wasn't a civilian?" Nash asked, his brows snapping together.

"It's different when you're with a club. But with you, I don't think your being in or out would have really made a difference to me," Ares said.

A growly sound came from Zayne, making Nash look up at him. Zayne was glaring at Ares. Was that jealousy he saw there? Nash bit his lip to keep from smiling. He took Zayne's hand, pulling him toward the door.

"I think we need to talk. You know, about the whole 'old man' thing," Nash said.

"Sure, go *talk* about it," Ares said and winked at him.

Zayne

With a hand on the small of Nash's back, he led him back to his room. They stepped inside and Zayne closed the door after them.

"We *should* talk about what this means," Zayne said.

Nash nodded and sat down on the bed, patting the seat next to him. Zayne walked to the bed and sat down, turning toward Nash.

"If we do this, you'll be mine," Zayne said.

Nash nodded. "Okay."

"You realize that in my world, this is the equivalent of being married, right?"

"Yeah. I get that," Nash said.

"And you're okay with that?"

Nash nodded and took Zayne's hand, rubbing his thumb over Zayne's still-bruised knuckles.

"I was miserable after we broke up. It felt like I'd lost a part of myself. Something Len said made me realize that I made the decision not to be a part of your world because of one incident where I didn't even have all the details. Len said you wouldn't have hurt him unless he deserved it. What did he do?"

Zayne didn't even entertain the idea of not telling Nash. There was no point. If they were going to make this work, he knew he needed to be more transparent about what happened at the club. He needed to include Nash.

"He was a Henchman and we needed information from him," Zayne said. When Nash opened his mouth, Zayne cut him off. "That's all I can tell you. You have to trust me. Trust that I'll tell you what I can. I know it won't be easy and I promise, if there's anything concerning you, me, or us, I'll tell you. But other than that, it's club business and that's for members only."

"I trust you," Nash said, squeezing Zayne's hand.

Zayne's lips quirked at the corners.

"I don't think you know how much I've wanted to hear that. How much I need it."

"What you told me last night? It made me realize that you were trusting me with much more than your own life." A smile spread on Nash's lips. "I'm glad I wasn't wrong about what kind of man you are."

Zayne's lips quirked into a smile and he leaned close to press his lips to Nash's. The kiss was sweet and short but conveyed everything he felt for Nash.

When he pulled back, he looked into Nash's eyes and said, "You know you have to wear a cut with 'Property of Saint' written on it?"

Nash frowned. "I can't wear that to work."

"You only have to wear it around the club, which includes Len's auto shop," Zayne said with a wry smile.

"I think I can manage that."

"Good. Then I have to go talk to the others," Zayne said.

"You think they'll agree to let him go?"

"I hope so."

Zayne raised their hands to press a kiss to Nash's palm. They shared a smile and then he let go. He stood and took two steps toward the door but was halted by fingers wrapping around his wrist. He glanced over his shoulder, meeting Nash's eyes.

"I didn't agree to this just to save Ares. You know that, right?"

Zayne turned. "Then why did you do it?"

"Well, it *was* to save him, but I also want to. I want to be yours. I love you."

He cupped Nash's cheeks and looked into his eyes as he said, "I love you, too."

The smile on Nash's face made his heart soar. Having that man love him felt like he was sure it would feel if he'd won the lottery. He was lucky. So damned lucky.

He walked downstairs and after asking one of the prospects for King's whereabouts, he headed for the man's office. He made his way across the courtyard, only stopping long enough to say hi to Hawk who must've just returned from his run. He walked into the garage and knocked on King's door before stepping into his office.

"Hey, King? I need a word."

King looked up from the documents in front of him and waved Zayne inside. Zayne closed the door and when he turned, King was walking around his desk, a serious expression on his face.

"Why do I have a feeling you're going to say something I won't like?"

"Probably because I am," Zayne said and straightened to his full height. "I owe Ares."

King crossed his arms over his chest and leaned against his desk, watching Zayne with perceptive eyes.

"And how is that exactly?"

"He saved Nash."

He wasn't going to mention Nash's half-threat of going to the cops. That wouldn't do anything but get Nash thrown off the property.

King arched an eyebrow at him. "Ares risks his life for a civilian and somehow that means you owe him?"

"Nash isn't a civilian. He's mine," Zayne said, leaving no room for misinterpretation.

King breathed a deep sigh. He laid a hand on Zayne's shoulder and squeezed gently.

"Well, hell. Why the fuck not?"

Zayne shifted his weight from one foot to the other, perturbed by how easily King had taken it.

"You're not going to argue with me? Tell me I'm an idiot?"

"No. But I'm not letting him go out of the goodness of my heart," King said with a pointed look.

Zayne nodded. "I know. I wouldn't have expected you to. But I also have a feeling we'll be able to use Ares."

"How so?"

"He wants out. Hell, he might even want in here."

He wasn't going to out Ares. With just about anything else, he would've thrown the asshole under the bus, but having experienced what being outed could do to someone, he couldn't bring himself to do it.

"I might only know this guy from his reputation and it's one hell of a bloody one, too, but I'm not willing to take him in. That's too big of a risk. Even for me," King said.

"I only said he might want in because we can use that against him."

"You think he'll be willing to work for us?"

"Yes," Zayne said without a doubt. "I think he's more than willing. I think he wants to stop Ronin from doing more harm."

"Well, we certainly should be able to use that," King said and rubbed his chin. He looked thoughtful for a long moment before he said, "He'll do more good on the inside."

"I'll ask him what he wants to do," Zayne said.

"He'll need a damned good cover story."

"No. He just needs to escape."

King arched a brow at him. "How do you suggest we make that believable?"

From what he understood, Ares hadn't told anyone he wanted out or that he disapproved of Ronin's way of running things. He knew Ares possessed the skills to escape captivity. He wasn't blind to the fact that the man hadn't even tried yet, and he knew King wasn't either.

"Put him with the other Henchman and let them escape," Zayne said.

"He'll have a somewhat credible witness," King said.

Zayne nodded. No one had seen Ares surrender to them when they'd gone to save Nash. If someone had, he didn't doubt they would've opened fire on all of them. That was the kind of club Ronin was running. With the guy they'd caught weeks ago, at least it was one person who could say Ares had escaped instead of being let go.

"Gimme a few hours to get everything set up," King said.

Zayne gave him a nod. He needed to have a lengthy chat with a certain Henchman anyway.

Chapter Sixteen

Zayne

HAVING NASH behind him again as they rode his bike was an amazing feeling. He hadn't realized just how much he'd missed it. Nash's head was leaned against his shoulder and his arms were wrapped around his waist.

He pulled up in front of Nash's building far too soon. If Nash hadn't needed to go home because he had work early the next morning, he would've kept Nash in his bed for much longer. Nash's arms disappeared and he got off. Zayne took off his helmet. Two bikes pulled up on either side of them, but Zayne ignored them in favor of watching Nash. There was a glow to his man, like his happiness was shining from him. He noticed Nash glancing at his brothers.

"They're just here for your protection," Zayne said.

"I know. It still feels weird."

Zayne dismounted and pulled Nash into his arms. Nash wrapped his arms around the back of Zayne's neck and looked up into his eyes.

"It's just until I know you're safe. You won't even see them."

Nash looked like he might argue for a second before he exhaled deeply and nodded. Zayne took his hand and walked with him to his front door. Nash unlocked his door and opened it, then he turned, his head tilted to the side as he ran his eyes down Zayne's body.

"You sure you can't stay?"

A smile fought to break free on Zayne's lips.

"Positive. I have to get back to the club," Zayne said.

Nash pursed his lips, nodding his head slowly. Zayne pulled a phone out of his pocket. He held it out to Nash.

"I thought you might want this back."

Nash cocked a brow, taking the phone and looking at it quizzically. "You got my phone back?"

"Jack and Sully got it from the van they'd taken you in," Zayne said.

"I dropped it in there, but they didn't notice."

"That's a good thing 'cause we used it to track you."

Nash's eyes went wide, and he asked, "You can do that?"

"Auggie can."

"Well, hell. I'd better thank him then," Nash said.

"I need to go," Zayne said.

Nash nodded but he didn't look happy about it. Zayne reached out to cup Nash's cheeks and pressed a kiss to his lips. Nash tried to deepen the kiss, pushing his body against Zayne's. He stepped back, breaking the kiss and shaking his head at Nash.

"Baby," Zayne warned. "I have to go and if you do that, I won't be leaving for hours."

Nash sighed, a cheeky smile finding his lips. "Worth a try."

Zayne waited until Nash was inside the apartment, door closed and locked, before he walked down the stairs and out of the building. Viper and Slasher were waiting by their bikes. He walked up to them and wasn't surprised when Slasher stepped forward.

"We won't let anything happen to him, brother," Slasher said.

Zayne laid a hand on Slasher's shoulder.

"I know."

"You just go take care of business. We'll keep an eye out for the Henchmen," Viper said, a smile playing on his lips. "I wouldn't mind having a little fun with them."

Viper was one of the enforcers and he'd gotten his road name because he was the kind of guy you never saw coming. Viper struck before you knew what was happening. He knew Nash would be safe with him around.

Zayne got on his bike and took off back to the clubhouse. They needed to figure things out with Ares and fast. Ares had agreed to be their inside man and to work with them to take down Ronin. It had taken a bit of convincing but if it hadn't, he wouldn't have believed Ares was really on their side.

There wasn't much traffic, so the drive didn't take long. He drove into the courtyard and parked his bike. He headed straight for the room they used for church. King, Addison, Joker, Auggie, and Ares were already there. Their conversation came to a halt as he walked into the room and didn't begin again until he was seated.

"I need to know exactly what it is you want from me," Ares said, a hard expression falling over his face. "I'm not selling out my brothers."

"I'm not asking you to," King said.

Ares let out a huff. "Sounds like you are."

"We all want Ronin out of the game. Let's focus on that," Joker said.

Ares' eyes shifted to Joker and after a moment of contemplating, Ares nodded and said, "I might not be alone in wanting him out of the club."

"You think there are others who feel the same as you?" Zayne asked.

"Yes. I can almost guarantee it."

"Good," King said. "You're gonna need those people. We all are."

"You get your brothers together, find the ones who want to defect and we'll help you do it," Addison said.

"That I can agree to," Ares said.

"Have we established a way to communicate?" Zayne asked King.

King raised his brows and turned to Auggie. It took Auggie a few seconds to realize they were all waiting for him to answer.

"Yes, sorry," Auggie blurted. He pulled out a black phone and handed it to Ares. "I've put an encryption software on it and as soon as you've sent a message, it codes it and when you receive a message from us, you'll only be able to read it once before it deletes itself."

Ares looked a bit surprised but also impressed.

"That's some crazy level of skills you've got there," Ares said.

"Thank you," Auggie said, a shy smile on his lips.

They went over a few more details before they got to the part of Ares and Clay's escape. They needed to be careful. There was no way King would go through with any plan that could endanger his men and women.

"No guns," Addison said.

"What about the guard? Clay will think something's off if he doesn't have one tonight," Ares said.

"We can't risk that," Zayne said. "He can have an unloaded gun. But then you *have* to be the one to take it from him."

Ares nodded and said, "I can do that."

"Good. We'll put Hawk or Reaper as the guard. They both know how to take care of themselves in risky situations," King said.

"Let's do this, then," Joker said.

"It has to be tonight," Addison said. She glanced at Ares. "We can't risk holding Ares any longer. Ronin is probably planning an attack as we speak."

"I agree," Ares said with a nod at Addison. "I'm his VP, even if I regret that, and he's definitely putting a plan together to free me."

Auggie pushed back his chair and stood. "I guess there's only one thing left to decide on." Auggie glanced at Ares. "Rope or handcuffs?"

For a second, Zayne's brain went into the gutter and from the look on Addison's face, so did hers.

"You know how to get out of either?" King asked.

"If I have something to work with, I can get out of the handcuffs easier."

"Do we even have handcuffs?" Addison asked.

Auggie chuckled and said, "From what I've heard, Joker has one hell of a collection."

Joker flipped him off and growled, "Fuck you, Band-Aid."

"No thank you, I'm not into bondage."

Zayne motioned for Ares to follow him and they left while Auggie and Joker bickered, much to Addison's amusement. King was simply watching them with heavy disapproval. Ares quickly fell in step with Zayne as he led the way to the second floor.

"You need to do everything you can to keep them from retaliating," Zayne said.

"I won't let them hurt Nash."

Zayne came to an abrupt halt and turned to Ares. "That's not what I said."

"I know."

Zayne clenched his teeth to keep from saying anything and resumed walking.

"If you get Clay to admit to being the one who told us about the drugs, he's not gonna talk about anything he might think strange or suspicious about tonight. Not if you promise to keep it a secret."

"I didn't know they'd moved the damned drugs here," Ares grumbled. He shook his head. "I was there because I thought the idiots had stolen it, only to find out they'd acted on Ronin's orders. Then you guys showed up. What did you do with it?"

Zayne pressed his lips together, fighting a smile. "Gave it to the cops."

"Well, damn," Ares said, a grin on his face as he shook his head.

Zayne stopped close to the room they were keeping Clay in and turned to Ares.

"Phone?"

Ares pulled the cellphone out of his pocket. He laid it in Zayne's hand.

"I'll make sure the guard has it on him," Zayne said.

Auggie found them shortly after, carrying a pair of handcuffs. He handed them to Zayne who motioned for Ares to turn around. He put the cuffs around Ares' wrists and then turned Ares back around.

"What do you need to get out of these?" Zayne asked.

"Don't worry. I've got what I need."

"Disconcerting, but all right. Let's do this," Auggie said.

Auggie led the way to the room they kept Clay in, Ares walking next to Zayne, a far off look on his face. Trusting Ares didn't come easy, but after seeing the way he was with Nash, seeing that other side to a man he'd only known through his reputation, he was convinced Ares wanted Ronin gone as much as he did.

Reaper was the one standing outside the door. When he saw them, he started toward them. Zayne gave Ares a last look and stepped back, letting Reaper grab a hold of Ares' arm. He heard King step up behind him and glanced over his shoulder. King's gaze was on Ares and Reaper, not moving until they both disappeared into the room. King turned his attention on Zayne, a smile gracing his lips.

"I guess we'd better call a vote on your man," King said.

Zayne nodded, his lips twitching. There needed to be a vote held on Nash becoming his old man. It also needed to be unanimous. He was a bit apprehensive about that. Bullet might not feel too great about having Nash back around after he screwed up last time. He didn't know how Addison had disciplined him, but he knew how brutal she could be. There was a reason she was the sergeant at arms; no one wanted to cross her. She kept everyone following the bylaws, though he was sure some only did it to stay on her good side.

"Don't worry. No one will vote against seeing you happy," King said.

"Let's hope that's true. I can't give him up again. I won't."

"I know love when I see it, Saint, and trust me, I'll be the last guy to stand in your way."

He'd only heard about the struggles King and Polly went through when they first got together but he knew it'd been tough. Having King on his side in this meant a lot to him.

Nash

It was a busy day at work, and he was just fine with that. He didn't get much time to think about the two bikers following him everywhere or the other bikers who might come back for him. It was still there, in the back of his mind, though. But two car crashes, one heart attack, and a child who'd fallen from a swing set had kept Mel and him busy.

When their shift was over, they went to the locker room and changed out of their uniforms. He was putting on his shoes when Harper sat down on the bench across from him. He looked up and raised a brow at her.

"You seem happier," she said.

Nash shrugged and said, "Maybe I am."

"Why?" Harper asked and narrowed her eyes at him.

"You guys ready?" Mel asked, saving Nash from answering.

Mel grabbed Harper's hand and pulled her to her feet. She kissed her girlfriend before pulling her toward the door.

"Come on, we have reservations for six and we have to go home and change first. I do not want to be late," Mel said.

Harper groaned and glanced over her shoulder at Nash.

"We're going out for dinner with her parents," Harper said, pulling a face.

Mel slapped a hand to Harper's arm and gasped. "You dare make that face because of my family."

Harper rubbed her arm and said, "I love you, but having dinner with your parents always ends with twelve of your aunts and uncles, seven cousins, and everyone's kids joining us."

Nash couldn't help his laugh and wasn't surprised when he heard Caleb's chuckle from the other side of the lockers. Caleb walked around the corner.

"Better get used to it, Holland," Caleb said to Harper.

Harper flipped him off which only made Caleb and Nash laugh more. Mel pulled Harper toward the door before she could do or say anything else. Nash stood and grabbed his bag from his locker. Caleb already had his slung over his shoulder and he was waiting by the door for Nash. They walked out together, catching up to Mel and Harper in the garage. They were all headed for Harper's car, having carpooled that morning. They all lived within twenty minutes of the firehouse and after Caleb moved in with his boyfriend, he now lived even closer.

"Um, is there something you haven't told me?" Harper asked, her gaze over Nash's shoulder.

He frowned at her before turning around. As soon as his eyes landed on Zayne who was on his bike by the curb, a wide smile split his face. Zayne's eyes met his and Zayne was off his bike and striding toward him the next second. Nash bit his lip as he watched Zayne, admiring his sexy man.

Zayne stopped in front of him, cupping his cheeks and slamming his mouth over Nash's. Zayne's lips and tongue did delicious things to Nash. He held on and gave as good as he got. He slid his fingers into Zayne's hair, holding on tightly, just the way he knew Zayne liked it.

Zayne let him up for air when a loud whistle sounded. They turned to see Mel fanning herself.

"Hot damn. I forgot how sexy men can be," Mel said.

"Hey," Harper exclaimed, bumping her shoulder against her girlfriend's.

Mel laughed and winked at Nash. He grinned right back at her.

"You two back together, then?" Harper asked, her gaze on Zayne.

Nash looked up at Zayne, a sparkle in his eyes.

"Yes. We are."

Before they could start grilling him and Zayne for details, he pulled Zayne with him toward his bike. "I'll see you guys tomorrow," he said with a wave.

They walked to Zayne's bike and he took the helmet Zayne handed him with a smile on his lips. When Zayne was on the bike, he slid on behind him. The bike came to life with a quiet roar and then Zayne drove off. Nash closed his eyes, enjoying the rumbling machine between his legs and the wind blowing against them. He liked how free he felt when they rode. Liked the danger, too. It made him sure he was a bit of an adrenaline junkie, but only where Zayne was concerned.

When they walked into his apartment, he turned to Zayne and asked, "Ares?"

Zayne nodded and said, "He made his *escape* with his buddy last night. We followed them to make sure they got to York without incident. Ares gave us confirmation three hours ago."

Nash cocked his head to the side and frowned at Zayne.

"I thought you weren't going to share club secrets with me," Nash said.

Zayne reached for him, putting his hands on Nash's arms. "I told you, if it's to do with you or us, I will always tell you. As much as I hate to admit it, Ares has to do with you."

Nash felt a smile widen his lips. He ran his hands down Zayne's chest, looking up at him.

"If you're worried I'll leave you for some other handsome biker, don't be. You're all I need, baby. All I want is you."

"You think he's handsome?"

"That's all you got from what I just said?" Nash asked.

He shook his head and dropped his hands, taking a step back. Zayne moved with him and caught his hands, putting them back on his chest.

"I can't wait for you to get your cut," Zayne growled.

"Why?"

"It'll tell everyone not only that you're taken but to stay the hell away from you."

Nash felt a frown form on his forehead. "What if I don't want people to stay away? Can't I talk to Gabe and Jet? What about Auggie? Or Len?"

"You're pretty cute, you know that?"

Nash wrinkled his nose. "No."

"What I meant is that the property patch is a warning to others. It tells them that you're off limits," Zayne said.

"Wouldn't they know that already? I mean, you told everyone, right?"

"Everyone at *my* club, yes. But we don't just stay here, we meet up with other clubs from time to time." Zayne shook his head with a grunt. "I need to teach you about being in a motorcycle club."

"Well, I guess that'd be a pretty good idea seeing as I'm now a part of one."

"You're not a member, baby."

"No, I'm just semi-married to one."

Zayne's smile was wide, and Nash couldn't help himself from pressing his lips to Zayne's.

Chapter Seventeen

Nash

THEY WERE sitting outside the firehouse in lawn chairs, enjoying the sun. They were nearing the end of their shift and, thankfully, it'd been an uneventful day. It'd been a few weeks since the whole kidnap, rescue, and then becoming Zayne's old man. Being with Zayne was so much better than he'd imagined. Knowing that Zayne wanted him to be a part of his life and knowing exactly what that life entailed, had given him a peace of mind he hadn't known he needed. He didn't know everything that went on in the club, but that didn't bother him. He knew what they all stood for now and that was mainly helping people in need. Even though there might be a way to help those people in a more legal way, he knew they'd probably be safer with the Kings compared to the cops. Talyssa was an obvious example of that.

"Twenty minutes," Caleb said and shifted his head on the back of his chair to look at Nash. "Got any plans?"

"Right now I wish I didn't, so I could just sit here all day," Nash said.

Caleb grinned at him and he felt a smile spread on his own lips.

"Your boyfriend picking you up?"

"Yeah," Nash said, closing his eyes as he turned his face back toward the sun.

"I still can't believe you're dating someone with a motorcycle and that you ride on it," Caleb said.

"What can I say. I like a little danger in my life."

A lot more than his colleagues knew of. He'd told his parents and Harper about Zayne being a King. Surprisingly, they'd all been more or less alright with it. A bit shocked and skeptical, but they'd all come to love Zayne and saw him as part of the family. And because Harper knew, Mel knew, too. They were both fine with it. Or as Harper had said it; she was good with at least some of the criminals in the city being somewhat on their side. He was still getting used to the club, though. It wasn't that different from working at the firehouse, as most of them were bonded through heart-wrenching and dangerous experiences and they were all one big family. He liked that about it.

Then there were things like his cut. It had taken a while for it to be made but once he'd finally gotten it, he'd rarely taken it off, not unless he'd had to. The back had 'Property of Saint' printed on it. He knew he wasn't actually a piece of property, Zayne made sure of that, but he loved everything wearing a cut with Zayne's name on it stood for. It meant that he was Zayne's, but it also meant that Zayne was his.

Zayne never wore his cut to the firehouse. With Nash's job being what it was, they didn't want to arouse suspicion. According to his contract, he was free to date whoever he wanted, but being with an outlaw biker probably wouldn't go over very well with the higherups.

His mom had been worried in the beginning which was why he hadn't told her about being kidnapped. She would've freaked out and killed him for almost getting killed. That was her logic, not his. He hadn't told Alanna either, knowing she'd make good on her threat to call the cops on Zayne, even though what happened wasn't really his fault.

Caleb's groan as he pushed out of his chair caught Nash's attention. A glance at the clock on his phone showed that there were five minutes left of their shift. Nash stretched his arms over his head and stood, hoping they didn't get called out in the last second.

Five minutes later, when Zayne pulled up in front of the firehouse, Nash was ready and waiting. He tried to make a clean escape, but Zayne was getting off his bike just as Harper and Mel came out of the firehouse.

"Hey, biker boy," Harper yelled.

Nash groaned and pulled a face. Zayne didn't look the least bit worried as he took his helmet off and left it on the seat of the bike. He ignored Harper in favor of grabbing Nash and bringing their mouths together in a soft kiss. Nash held on to Zayne's upper arms, a silly grin on his face when Zayne pulled back. Zayne was grinning right back at him, happiness shining from him. He'd never thought being with someone could be so fulfilling, that it would make him so happy. Zayne had become his home and even though it had all happened so fast, he'd never doubted his feelings for the man. He'd run scared once and he didn't intend to make that mistake again.

"Auntie Adisa said to tell you she's making dinner tomorrow night and you'd better be there," Harper said.

Nash rolled his eyes. "If she wanted us to come for dinner, she could've just asked us."

Harper snorted and said, "Boy, she did. You're just too far up biker boy's ass to check your damned phone."

"We'll be there," Zayne said and took Nash's hand in his, pulling him away.

Nash went willingly, waving and yelling goodbye to the others before turning to walk with Zayne to the bike. When they reached it, Zayne squeezed his hand before letting go. He took the helmet Zayne held out for him and pulled it over his head. He got behind Zayne on the bike and scooted forward until he was plastered against Zayne's back. It was one of the things he loved most about riding; being so close to Zayne. That and how free he always felt.

They were going to a barbecue at the club and it wasn't long before they drove up to the clubhouse. The gates swung open for them. As soon as they were both off the bike, Zayne pulled their cuts out of the saddlebag. Nash took his with a wry smile and put it on.

They found Auggie standing by the row of bikes, looking lost.

"What's wrong?" Nash asked as they walked up to him.

Auggie looked up, his lip jutting out in a pout. "I've been banned from the grill."

It was a struggle not to laugh at Auggie. He looked miserable.

"What did you do this time?" Zayne asked.

"Nothing," Auggie grumbled.

"Why don't I believe you?" Nash asked as he slung an arm over Auggie's shoulders.

Together, they walked into the backyard. There was a tiny deck back there. It was just big enough for two grills and the guy manning them. The backyard was filled with chairs and people. He was still learning everyone's names and while he'd learned pretty quickly that they were all kind and forgiving people, he still felt bad when he didn't get it right. Also, a lot of the guys were big, bearded, and burly so he tended to stay with either Auggie, Gabe, or Len. Them, or the guys from the auto shop.

Auggie led him toward a corner of the lawn where Gabe was lying on a picnic blanket while Nic, Sully, Len, and Jet were sitting in chairs around it. As they walked, he glanced around, trying to see if he could remember who was who. He recognized the president, King, who was standing by the grill with a woman next to him. He couldn't really place her, but he figured she was probably King's wife and Gabe's mother.

Zayne told him he was going to go get them something to eat and Nash just nodded, continuing toward the others with Auggie.

"Didn't my dad throw you out?" Gabe asked, shielding his eyes from the sun with his hand as he looked up at Auggie.

Auggie grumbled something under his breath and went to sit down in a chair. Nash got down to sit next to Gabe on the blanket. Gabe sat up and wrapped his arms around his legs, resting his chin on his knees.

"How does one manage to get thrown out of here?" Nash asked.

Gabe grinned. "By setting my mom's steak on fire and then throwing it across the lawn."

Nash pulled a face. Yeah. He could see how that'd put Auggie on King's bad side. He sat back, resting on his hands. Zayne returned shortly after and handed Nash a plate. Zayne sat down in one of the chairs to eat. Nash ate while talking to Gabe who stole a few fries off his plate. Gabe and Len were the two people at the club he felt the most connected to, apart from Zayne. They both managed to put him at ease.

The barbecues were members only, which meant the scantily clad women who frequented the clubhouse weren't there. He wasn't really sure he'd get used to them. As Zayne had explained it, they were called club bunnies and were either there just to have sex or for a chance at becoming a club member's old lady. There were still many things he didn't know or didn't understand, but one thing he'd learned about these people was that they considered each other family, and he doubted there was anything they wouldn't do for each other.

"I heard Wildcat's been complaining about you disappearing during your shifts at the gym," Jet said with a brow cocked at Zayne.

Zayne groaned and flipped Jet off. Gabe and Jet laughed. Nash bit his lip and glanced up, meeting Zayne's darkening gaze. He'd been to the gym with Zayne twice to watch him teach a few classes. He hadn't expected seeing Zayne all sweaty and beating people up would turn him on as much as it did. He shouldn't have been surprised when they'd ended up finding the nearest empty spot to get off after Zayne was finished with his classes.

Zayne

When he and Nash were finished with their dinners, he grabbed Nash's plate and walked into the kitchen with both. Inside he found Jordan and Maya busy washing dishes. Jordan groaned loudly when he saw Zayne.

"Really? There's more?" Jordan complained.

Zayne chuckled. "You're lucky I'm not Joker or you would've gotten yourself more work to do for complaining."

"Fuck," Jordan said, shaking his head.

Zayne handed Jordan the plates and patted him on the shoulder. He left them to it and walked back outside. He stopped by the table with drinks, his eyes landing on Nash who was laughing and joking around with Gabriel. He turned his head when he felt someone walk up behind him.

"He's adjusting quite well, isn't he?" Addison asked.

Zayne couldn't help his smile as he watched Nash flip off Jet. "He is. He's liking it a lot more than I ever thought he could."

"He fits," Addison said.

He turned his gaze on Addison.

"I like him with hair," Addison said, a smile teasing her lips.

Zayne's lips twitched and he said, "Me too."

Addison waggled her brows at him and left to join the others. She sat down on the blanket and slung an arm around Nash's shoulders. Two seconds later, Nash was pushing her away, his laughter reaching Zayne's ears.

"You know you're allowed to do more than just look, right?"

Zayne's lips quirked as he turned to his best friend. Joker was watching him with an amused look in his eyes.

"Shut up."

Joker threw up his hands. "I'm just saying."

"Where's Gabe?" Zayne asked.

Joker gave him a nasty glare.

"Don't start with that again."

"You know he wants you," Zayne said.

"Yeah, he's been quite loud about that, thanks to you, no doubt. You asshole."

Zayne shook his head, glancing down to hide the smile on his face. Joker was going to have his work cut out for him where Gabe was concerned. Now that Joker had finally realized that Gabe was into him, Gabe wasn't going to back down. The kid was used to fighting for what he wanted. Getting Joker wasn't going to be any different.

"Have you heard from our Henchman?" Joker asked.

Zayne nodded and turned to him as he said, "Everything is going smoothly. Apparently, there are plenty who are sick and tired of Ronin. Not that I blame them. I knew he was crazy but from what Ares has told me, he's lost his fucking mind."

"Has King figured out what he wants to do with these people?"

"Besides using them against Ronin? I don't think so."

"I think we can use them for more than just that," Joker said.

"I'm sure you'll come up with something. It's why you're the VP."

"That and I'm good at making people do what I want. Except for you. And Gabe, apparently."

Zayne looked at Joker with pretend shock. "What? You not enjoying your new roommate-situation?"

"Fuck you," Joker growled.

Zayne chuckled and turned his gaze back on Nash. He tilted his head to the side as Nash bent over, his eyes on Nash's firm ass. He loved that ass. It was all his. Fingers snapping in front of his face made him tear his eyes away from Nash.

Gash was looking at him with a smirk. Zayne glanced around himself, finding Joker gone.

"Man, you're completely under his spell, aren't you?"

Zayne scoffed and returned his eyes to Nash. Maybe he *was* under a spell, and if he was, he never wanted it broken. He left Gash behind and headed toward Nash, desire thrumming through his blood.

Nash

He wasn't surprised to see heat in Zayne's eyes. The way the man made his way toward him made him feel like prey and he didn't mind. Not one bit. He moved slowly toward the house, angling to get Zayne away from everyone. He only just made it inside when Zayne caught up with him. Arms wrapped around his waist, pulling him back against a muscular chest. Zayne's lips grazed Nash's ear before moving to that spot below it.

"You trying to hide from me?" Zayne asked in a husky voice that sent shivers down Nash's spine.

There were a few people sitting on the couches in the clubhouse but none of them paid them any attention. Nash turned, pulling out of Zayne's arms and walked backwards. He wore a mischievous grin as he began to unbutton his shirt.

"Upstairs," Zayne growled.

Nash turned on his heels and ran up the stairs, heading for Zayne's room. It was one thing he really liked about the clubhouse. Having their own private room. He opened the door and stepped inside, heading straight for the bed. He sat down and pulled off his shoes and socks, knowing he wouldn't have time once Zayne got a hold of him. Zayne stepped through the door, closing and locking it behind him.

Zayne walked right up to him and pulled him to his feet, slamming his mouth over Nash's. Zayne's tongue pushed past his lips, owning him in a way no one ever had before. Nash groaned and grabbed onto Zayne's shoulders, his knees going weak.

When they came up for air, Nash slid his hands under Zayne's shirt. Zayne buried his nose in Nash's hair.

"I love your hair," Zayne said.

"I've noticed."

Letting it grow out had turned out to be a damned good idea. Especially with how much Zayne was loving it and how much it turned out he liked it when Zayne pulled on it during sex. Normally, he hated when people touched his hair, but Zayne? He could do whatever he wanted to him and he'd love every second of it.

Nash shrugged out of his cut to pull his shirt off. The shirt hit the floor, but he kept the cut in one hand. He looked up, meeting Zayne's eyes.

"Keep it on?" he asked, knowing full well what Zayne's answer would be.

"Keep it on," Zayne growled.

He put it back on, loving the dark look in Zayne's eyes as he watched him. He reached into his back pocket, grabbing the packet of lube there. He pushed it into Zayne's hand. Zayne gave him a heated look.

"Came prepared, did you?"

Nash grinned as he shrugged, saying, "I know you."

Zayne got Nash out of his pants and then he took Nash's mouth in a kiss. He walked Nash backwards, then pulled back and turned him around. Zayne pushed him against the window, his lips moving down the side of Nash's neck. Nash shivered with lust and moaned when Zayne slipped his lube-slick fingers between his cheeks.

Zayne circled his hole before pressing a finger inside. Nash groaned, his grip on the windowsill tightening. There was nothing slow or tentative about the way Zayne got him ready. Zayne didn't waste any time adding another finger. He pumped his fingers into Nash who was gasping and moaning while he pushed back on Zayne's fingers.

"Fuck," Nash panted. "I need you. Need you inside me. Now."

Zayne

Nash's hands were on the glass and he was pushing his ass out as he arched his back. He was so damned beautiful when he let go like that.

Zayne removed his fingers and unzipped his pants, pulling them down to free his cock. He ripped open a condom packet and rolled the condom down his hard length. With one hand on Nash's hip, he pushed into Nash's tight hole, groaning at the amazing feeling of being inside Nash. He waited for Nash to adjust around him. He slid his hands up Nash's chest, reaching for his nipples. He tweaked them, teasing them into hard points. Nash groaned and pushed his ass against Zayne, but he didn't move. Nash cursed, then pulled his hips forward to push back, fucking himself on Zayne's cock, over and over. He let Nash play around for a while, loving the sounds Nash made, loving the slide of his cock inside him.

"Baby," Nash begged.

Zayne grabbed Nash by the hips and thrust into him, setting a hard pace he knew Nash loved. The needy sounds coming from Nash drove him wild. He glanced down, the white letters on Nash's cut standing out against the black leather. He loved seeing his name on Nash's cut. Loved when Nash wore it.

He grabbed Nash by the chin, forcing him to look out the window. He pressed a kiss to the side of Nash's neck, then said, "You see them?"

Nash groaned, nodding his head. They could see almost everyone in the backyard from there.

"They could look up any second and see how shameless you are. How much you want my cock."

He moved his hand to Nash's hair, tugging his head to the side so he could kiss, lick, and bite the side of his neck.

"Do you want them to see you, baby?"

"Fuck. Yes. Fuck," Nash panted. "I'm so close."

Zayne wrapped a hand around Nash's cock, jerking him off as he thrust into him. Nash only got louder, his words getting incoherent.

"You're mine, Nash. All mine," he said, fucking him harder.

Nash spilled all over the wall and windowsill, his ass tightening around Zayne's cock and sending him over the edge. His balls drew up and he shot into the condom, thrusting into Nash a few more times.

He leaned forward, putting a hand on the glass to hold himself up while he breathed heavily. He disposed of the condom and pulled his pants up. He wrapped his arms around Nash, pulling him close. Nash was still trembling from his orgasm. Zayne placed a kiss to Nash's cheek and moved him to the bed, making him sit down. Nash fell back onto the bed and let Zayne clean him up without a sound. He picked up Nash's clothes, placing them on the bed.

"You've ruined me," Nash mumbled.

"Huh?"

Nash pushed up on his elbows, his gaze meeting Zayne's. "You've completely ruined me for other guys."

Zayne narrowed his eyes at Nash and said, "There won't be any other guys."

Nash bit his lip, looking at Zayne with a wicked gleam in his eyes.

"God, I love it when you get jealous."

"Get dressed," Zayne growled. "Or we'll spend the whole night here and I'd rather take you home."

Nash chuckled and sat up to reach for his clothes. Zayne watched while Nash dressed, noting the way Nash was looking at him. They were definitely going to continue this later.

When Nash was ready, Zayne grabbed his hand. Nash smiled up at him.

"I love you," Nash said.

No matter how many times he heard Nash say the words, it never got old. He lowered his head to press their lips together.

"I love you, too, baby."

They walked back downstairs and out into the backyard. They made their way to the others and Zayne wasn't surprised when Addison ran her eyes over them.

"Don't you two look delightfully ruffled," Addison said, a smug smile on her face.

Zayne flipped her off before wrapping an arm around Nash and pulling him closer. Nash was staring down at his feet, so Zayne knew he was trying to hide his embarrassment. Nash wasn't the least bit shy when it was just the two of them, but he tended to get flustered around the others. Zayne was more than okay with that. It just meant that Nash trusted him completely and was a hundred percent himself with Zayne.

Zayne sat down while Gabe pulled Nash toward the table where they kept the drinks.

"Maybe you should try it," Zayne said to Addison.

"Try what? Having sex?" She snorted out a laugh. "I'm sorry to break it to you, sweetheart, but I've been doing that since I was seventeen."

Zayne shook his head. "Having sex with someone you care about. Or maybe someone your own age."

She raised a blonde eyebrow at him. "And why would I do that?"

"I just thought you might find that older guys tend to have more experience," Zayne said with a shrug.

"What if I like teaching?"

"Awe, come on, Stiletto," Jet said. "Give poor Jordan a chance. He might surprise you."

She flipped them both off and said, "Stay out of my sex life, assholes."

Gabe and Nash returned with enough beers to get them all drunk. Nash sat down in the chair next to Zayne's and handed him a beer. Rooster joined them, taking Len's chair so she could sit in his lap. Gabe and Nash were talking about

Washington when Nash trailed off. Zayne glanced over his shoulder, finding the reason standing there awkwardly. Joker's arms were crossed, and his eyes were on Nash.

"I'm glad you decided to stay," Joker said, surprising the hell out of everyone around him, including Zayne.

Nash's mouth fell open and he just stared at Joker.

"This idiot deserves to be happy," Joker said and put a hand on Zayne's shoulder.

"I love you, too," Zayne said.

Joker found a chair and sat with Zayne and Nash, proceeding to get Nash drunk with some stupid drinking game. Nash didn't usually drink that much but he was sure it had to do with wanting Joker's approval. If that was what it took for the two of them to get along, then he was all for it.

It was getting close to midnight when Zayne stood.

"Come on. Let's go home," Zayne said and took Nash's hand.

Nash smiled up at him and let Zayne pull him to his feet. Nash leaned in for a messy kiss. Zayne chuckled against his lips and pulled back.

"How much did you drink?" Zayne asked.

"Just enough," Nash said, his words slurred.

Zayne shook his head and wrapped an arm around Nash's waist. They said their goodbyes and then Zayne led Nash through the yard. When they reached the courtyard, Zayne let go of Nash and turned to him with a raised brow.

"You good to ride?"

Nash nodded and said, "I'm good. Take me home."

Home was now a rented townhouse close to the firehouse and Nash's parents. Staying in Nash's tiny apartment hadn't been ideal and there was no way they could stay at his place with Joker so as soon as Nash's lease was up, they'd found a place together. Joker hadn't been too happy about it but that was mostly due to his new roommate. He'd found the perfect renter. Gabriel had been more than happy to take the room. Getting out of his parents' house had been on his to-do list for a while. Zayne was hoping having Gabriel that close would open Joker's eyes to the possibility of getting some happiness for himself. The dumbass needed someone to care for him, even if he didn't think he did.

Zayne felt his lips quirk at the corners. Joker had been pissed at him for moving out and leaving him with Gabriel, but he seemed to have gotten over it. Zayne reached out to help Nash with his helmet. He closed the strap and grabbed his own helmet. Nash mumbled something under his breath.

"What's that?"

Nash's eyes darted up to meet Zayne's. "Nothing. I didn't say anything."

Zayne arched a brow at him and crossed his arms over his chest.

"Is that so?"

Nash shook his head, stopped, then nodded.

Zayne slapped Nash's ass and said, "Let's get your drunk ass home."

He swung a leg over the bike and settled onto the seat. Nash crawled on behind him and wrapped his arms tightly around Zayne's waist. Zayne started the bike and drove through the open gate onto the road. Heading home with Nash pressed against his back was the best damned feeling in the world.

Ana Night is a writer of suspenseful gay romance. She's an avid reader who has loved the written word since she discovered it. When she was a kid, she never went anywhere without a notebook. She was always writing, be it in the backseat of the car, between classes in school, or by the pool on vacations.

When she's not writing, you can find her with her nose buried in a book, singing and dancing, watching her favorite TV shows, or creating book covers.

Ana lives in Denmark where she spends most of her time running from her ninja kitty—that one goes for the ankles—and getting lost in the woods with her horse.

Website: www.ananight.com
Email: ana.night@outlook.com
Newsletter: www.eepurl.com/dBnBw1
Instagram: www.instagram.com/authorananight
Facebook: www.facebook.com/authorananight

Made in the USA
Las Vegas, NV
25 September 2021